The Mongolian Travel Guide

Svetislav Basara

THE MONGOLIAN TRAVEL GUIDE

Translated from the Serbian by Randall A. Major

DALKEY ARCHIVE PRESS

Originally published in Serbian by Dereta Publishing as *Mongolski bedeker* in 1998.

Copyright © by Svetislav Basara, 1998.
Translation copyright © by Randall A. Major, 2018.
First Dalkey Archive edition, 2018.
All rights reserved.

Library of Congress Cataloging-in-Publication Data

Names: Basara, Svetislav, 1953- author. | Major, Randall A., translator.
Title: The Mongolian Travel Guide / Svetislav Basara ; translated from the Serbian by Randall A. Major.
Other titles: Mongolski bedeker. English
Description: First Dalkey Archive edition. | McLean, IL : Dalkey Archive Press, 2018.
Identifiers: LCCN 2018027180 | ISBN 9781628972504 (pbk. : alk. paper)
Classification: LCC PG1419.12.A79 M6613 2018 | DDC 891.8/2354—dc23
LC record available at https://lccn.loc.gov/2018027180

Co-funded by the Creative Europe
Programme of the European Union

www.dalkeyarchive.com
McLean, IL / Dublin

The European Commission support for the production of this publication does not constitute an endorsement of the contents which reflects the views only of the author, and the commission cannot be held responsible for any use which may be made of the information contained therein.

Printed on permanent/durable acid-free paper

This book was supposed to be published in Sarajevo, in an edition of Svjetlosti Publishers. Before it was finished, Sarajevo was blanketed in absolute darkness. That is why I am dedicating it to all the victims.

Contents

The Name of the Rain

IF THE SPRING of that year, the Year of the Iron Dragon in the Chinese calendar, was old-fashioned—then the summer was eccentric. It snowed twice in July, and once the dawn never came, so the night lasted for forty-eight hours. And so on, day after day. Nothing happened. Just like in earlier years, when the summers were more respectable. Our tiny whims exist just to camouflage our desperate emptiness. I thought: when the time comes, I will have nothing to write about, and my next book, like the preceding ones, will be brimming with loneliness, boredom, and nullity. Now, it is possible that I wasn't thinking about that; I was gathering material for future works of fiction: an abundance of nausea, loads of fears, huge bins overflowing with feelings of failure and numbness—all the tedious material of modern storytelling. But I wrote nothing down. God is my witness. Suddenly, an interesting reason to write popped up. My friend, N. V., made sure of that. He committed suicide.

A classic: a hundred barbiturates and sliced veins. But that's still no kind of story line. What's strange about that, that one of my friends kills themselves? A year does not pass without two or three of them committing suicide. However, something was hanging in the air. I went to the funeral, suffered through one more attempt by those present to make an awful thing, such as death and the removal of the corpse, into a dignified act; I confirmed to myself that such attempts end in failure and headed home.

But I didn't get home. Not that quickly. At the exit to the cemetery I was joined by the priest, who, against the regulations of the Serbian Orthodox Church, had said the Mass for my deceased friend. He seemed familiar to me, but that meant nothing; all priests look alike, and once you meet one of them it's as if you've met them all. Yet there were some differences. This one was named Luke, like the evangelist, and to some extent he was one of the Fools for Christ. He invited me to go with him to a tavern on the way. "For one quick little shot," he said. We ordered the first drink that came to mind. I think it was rum.

Three or four hundred years ago, they would have impaled that priest on a stake, singed his beard, killed his dog, slaughtered his cow, and torn down his house. But now, in the Age of Enlightenment, the church dignitaries put up with him. They even showed him a certain benevolence. I think it would be better if they impaled him on a stake, because I hate the Age of Enlightenment. This anemic time in which everything has been researched, everything exposed, everything brought to light. But it's a well-known fact that the really great things are found in the darkness.

In order to believe the priest's story, in order to listen to him at all, I had to drink glass after glass of horrible JAMAICA rum. Anyway, I had a good excuse: I was mourning for my friend. The priest was drinking because of the prejudice that all priests like to get into the sauce. No one could accuse us of anything.

At some point, not believing himself in what he was saying, the priest started preaching. Fairly convincingly.

"Death," he said, "should not be feared. It is terrible just because it is, if I can say it that way, on the other side of the curtain. Life should be feared. Here the place is roiling with demons, witches, warlocks, evil spirits . . . And everyone keeps trying to prove that all those things are just superstitions. They are aided in that by fashion designers, the educational program on TV, makeup and perfume factories, producers of condoms and sexual aids, sexy lingerie designers . . . All of those who make their living by herding people into hell, which is a pointless job, because everyone is going to hell anyway, just deeper into it. Since 1796, no one has gone to heaven. Nor will they. It's closed. There are still a few free places in hell. Cupidity and video recorders have completely ruined the world. Everyone is just staring at screens from which, in silent intervals, undetectable by human senses, the messages of the devil's propaganda machine pour out."

Here, he paused. He drank down a glass of rum. He looked at my watch. Quite airy, like a wisp of steam rising from a hot sidewalk, he became partially transparent. Through his head one could see the open door of the tavern's kitchen and the guys cooking cattle heads in a cauldron.

"All right, the thing about television," I said, "that's more or less a well-known thing. But heaven? That's difficult to believe."

"It's difficult to believe in anything. And that's why things are the way they are. No one, for example, knows that Mitterrand is a robot, and that more than ninety percent of the politicians, bankers and employees of the OUN are just computer personalities, hologram creatures, three-dimensional quanta of nothingness."

I thought to myself—the priest has had a few too many. Or he, too, is one of those creatures he is talking about. A provocateur. Had I not just minutes before seen right through him, seen the specters skulking around the kitchen? At that very moment, the priest thought: far from it; holograms are even less transparent than the darkest of nights. Then he said aloud: what you saw, you didn't see it through me, rather a memory from long ago, common to us both, appeared between us. Perhaps he didn't say that out loud either. We were both pretty smashed, so my thoughts and his were liberated from the centripetal force of egotism—they were hovering freely above the table, intermingling with the wine gnats and making us believe that they were fireflies.

The priest looked at my watch again, even though he wasn't in a hurry to go anywhere. So, he said, "Let's go on drinking. That's the only way we'll save ourselves."

"But, didn't you just say that the number of the saved has been fulfilled, that Guf[1] is empty and that, in all of this, time is just waiting for the quota of the damned to be fulfilled."

"Yes, I did say that, but there is also one other possibility. It was written about by mystics from Syria. Those manuscripts were burned. They were reconstructed on the basis of the morphology of the remaining ashes, and in a nutshell they say: whoever is repulsed by the mire of this world and consciously destroys themselves, they can be saved, only of course if they don't end up in a delirium[2], or if they don't drink to enjoy themselves or to forget: the difference between a perfect bull's-eye and a complete miss is negligible. The subtler souls resort to alcohol not to enjoy themselves, but rather to crucify themselves, to search out the darkest corners of their reeking souls, to bring all their filth into the light of day, and completely raze the *ratio* to the ground. To make time stop. That's why I kept glancing nervously at

---

1 Guf, in Jewish and Christian mysticism, is the place where the souls of the unborn reside. When all the souls are born and receive their bodies, the first human being without a soul will be born, signifying the beginning of the Apocalypse. (From the film *The Seventh Seal*)

2 Delirium, it should be emphasized, is mistakenly treated as a psychological illness. In fact, it is the peak of sensory refinement, in which this world shows itself as it really is. Many are unable to withstand that insight, and about their further fate nothing is known for sure.

your watch, not because of what you might think later. Rather to see if time is stopping, whether it is slowing down to its proper speed . . . Does the flow have continuity? Does it look more like a wide, slow river or like a rushing mountain stream?"

Now I glanced at my watch. I didn't see anything. About this, I thought, the priest is right. But like a reflection in the mirror. It seemed that everything was that way, but everything was different, in a different place, and vice versa. All our truths are like that. And so is everything else. Because we aren't the ones who lend our faces to mirrors; rather mirrors shape our faces. Because we're turned toward the external. Once I read in an article about the achievements of medicine that doctors had found some sort of derivative of morphine or heroin, or even LSD, that's secreted by the brain; thus, we're practically always on a high—from which I draw the conclusion that everything we see is just a hallucination.

"Of course," the priest's thoughts sparkled in the swarm of wine gnats above the table, "that is why the church prescribes the fast. If you don't introduce fat into your organism, there is no material for creating those drugs and then you see things more clearly. The Creator acted humanely after all. For who could stand this world without anesthesia?"

As I headed to the restroom, I walked right through the priest. Without thinking. In his lethargy, he didn't even notice. I barely paid heed to that detail myself.

But, encouraged now, and wishing to walk through the closed door as well, I hit my head and almost fell down. This caused a roar of laughter among the patrons of the tavern. As just stated: the difference between a perfect bull's-eye and a complete miss is negligible. On my way back, I did walk through the closed door, but not through the priest. I ran into him. And this time, I did fall down. The entire tavern rocked with laughter.

"Oh, my," said the priest, "it's getting late. Time to go home."

We said our good-byes at the door of the tavern. I liked the priest, but he was not without faults. Even though he had a watch, he always looked at mine, just to save a miserable twenty seconds or so.

Two days later, while, in an enormous retrospective, one of that summer's boring rains was pouring down, the postman, soaked to the skin, brought me a letter. He downed the schnapps I offered him in a gulp, and went into my closet to change his clothes because he was just a stand-in character. And the schnapps was just tap water. I immediately recognized the neat handwriting of my friend. So dead, yet his letters were still reaching their addressees. Such futile efficiency! I was in no hurry to open the envelope; what could a corpse have to tell me? I attempted to figure out the name of the rain. Without success. With rains it's like with women: the most beautiful, the most magnificent, seen in passing just for an instant, you never learn their names.

But it couldn't be put off forever, so I tore the letter open.

I will not begin with the conventional Dear, *etc. The very thought of writing a letter before committing suicide is largely disgusting to me, but this is not a farewell letter; I would rather say it is a business letter. In the end of all things, I'm counting on the usual sloppiness of the Postal Service. I am certain that enough time will have passed before this letter reaches your hands, and by then I will already be in a safe place, in the ground.*

In a certain sense—I will not actually kill myself. Consistent with your doctrine, I will die the same day I kill myself (at least that's not hard), but I want to get a bit ahead of death, to make it come helter-skelter, to leave behind some job it's already started and come to finish me off. I'm writing these lines because some things can be said by a man when he's dead, and that, de jure, *I am. Life had not become unbearable for me; it always was in fact, as it is for everyone else, but despite its unbearableness, I never had any desire to kill myself and I decided in favor of that act for platonic reasons: I could have muddled through fifty more years without grumbling about it, and that tedium drove me to raise my hand against myself.*

Among other things, lately I'd been acting strangely toward everything. I found it hard to stomach that people still live in the erroneous belief that the earth is round, even though it's quite obvious it's flat. As you can see, the degree of tedium had advanced so far that there was every indication that I would one day enter the ranks of the profane and solemnly swear an oath of allegiance to the ordinary, which is a death even worse than suicide . . . There—even though I didn't intend to do so, I've begun to justify myself: one more piece of evidence corroborating the extent of my fall. Oh, if only the scholastics were still alive . . . What a treat for them. The best evidence of ancestral sin and the rottenness of our nature is indeed a justification, a daily justification for everything we do.

But don't let me waste your time, mine has run out anyway. Let's get down to work. Here's what this is all about. A month ago, a newly started magazine, Epoch, sent a proposal for me to travel to Mongolia and write a travel guide, or better said, an extended report on that godforsaken land. Since I'd already made my decision by then, I decided to propose that you go instead, and the executive officer agreed. Thus, thanks to my death, you'll see a bit of the world and I'll have the comfort of knowing that I did something useful.

Now, I'd like to say a thing or two about you. I could have done this while I was still alive, but why spoil such a rare friendship. Perhaps I could have just kept my opinion to myself. I hesitated, hand on my heart, whether I should give my opinion of you, but ultimately my idiotic genetic code demanding that I meddle spoke out, so I put you under the magnifying glass of my own achievements, not in order to humiliate you, but to urge you to start cleaning the Augean stables of your soul, whose existence I profoundly doubt.

Because, if anyone knows you, I do. Like Castor and

Pollux, we have muddled along since the mythological days of elementary school, to the Trojan Wars fought over provincial Helens (they were all bow-legged or knock-kneed, just a matter of percentages), over the search for the Golden Fleece of youth, up to the Kali Yuga of our mature years. Since I'm already using the language of myth, I have to say that you are Narcissistic. To say that you are Narcissus would be going too far. Incapable of communicating with your surroundings, you've built fabulous constructions of alienation and thus—with a veritable lake of ink—signed your own verdict liberating you from the responsibility of empathizing with, understanding, or helping others. You've even used agnosticism for that purpose. And so that the rare stings of the outside world wouldn't affect you, you became tolerant. What an incredible junk pile is keeping your personality intact. If you were honest in the least, you'd let them tattoo FRAGILE *on your forehead.*

You read books about the Golden Age, eat with your hands, and watch porno movies. You listen to black people's music in the safe exile of your room full of synthesizers, vials of toilette water, Red Army officers' caps, icons and axes, broken radios, and fortune cookies. To reckon with your fear of women, are you doing anything to overcome it, or are you going to join a monastery? No! You keep reading Schopenhauer and proclaim yourself to be a misogynist. Closed up in everything possible to close, you sit there and from your lair send out your miserable ultimatums to God.

In spite of it all, I always loved you.

Remain with God.

P. S.—
I was no better than you.

Well, there you go. Such things happen only in the years of the Steel Dragon. You get sent to Tunguska . . . No, Moldavia . . . No, Mongolia. As if that would give me eternal life. Is there any point in arguing with the dead? There isn't, but that's also true of the living, and yet we argue with them. Let's go ahead *ab ovo*. Why did he write me that letter? All right, that's his problem. It bothered him that people think the earth is round. That's indeed a sad story, my friend. Because of reprobates. Because of that awful type, an incomprehensible transgression got spread around. It's common knowledge the planet used to be a flat, square plate, but around six hundred years before Christ a disturbance occurred caused by that vertigo which Plato spoke of, a dizziness that is the consequence of our obsession with the curves of female buttocks. People started seeing everything as round. Boob-like. Ass-like. But that's no reason for a man to kill himself. Or is it? Or perhaps I, in some way, made my friend kill himself so that he would slap me in the face with the truth? No one could know for sure.

I tore the letter up just in case and went out into the street to freshen up, or rather to get rained on. A name-less rain, like those hundreds of specters whom I've seen hanging around bus stations and waiting rooms, specters who meant absolutely nothing except that they took up space and wandered about, spitting, just so they could dampen the emptiness and vacuity.

One more rain with no name.

But, as the ever-wise William of Baskerville would say: a name means nothing! That which is called rain would be just as wet and bothersome, and you would still feel just as miserable, unnecessary, and pitiful if it were called Margaux Hemingway or Susan Sontag.

Since the rain wasn't letting up, I set off down the dim streets of the town. Nothing ever happened to me there, either good or bad, but whenever I needed to go somewhere, I was overcome with nostalgia, and a deluge of fictitious memories would bring tears to my eyes. Where did that aporia come from? Perhaps I was just deceiving myself, thinking that in me there still remained a shred of humanity, and the tears were running down my face because of the sheer, ordinary horror of existence. Or perhaps because of conjunctivitis.

Although darkness had long since fallen, on the slopes of the surrounding hills the lights were just going on, forming a Zodiac circle of Electrification . . . The constellations of blacksmiths, bakers, and proletarians according to which, in the Golden Age of Renewal and Construction, the Party astrologers composed the horoscopes of the past.

In fact, since I have to be honest, I do have one memory here. Back in the day, I intended to pimp that memory out as well, because I wanted to write a film script that was doomed never to be made, so I didn't write anything. But it can't be ruled out that the memory itself was also inauthentic, I mean—that this didn't really happen and that the whole story is just a memory of the synopsis. But let's not overdo it, no one really has authentic memories. This is all about a memory of the opening of the first DEPARTMENT STORE.

I was perhaps five or six, or maybe ten, or even twenty; I was childish for a long time. Besides, back then time flowed according to decrees, and a day could end only if a bureaucrat somewhere put a stamp on it, a day could be extended only if the wheat still needed harvesting. Or until the Five-Year Plan was completed. Time itself had been nationalized, like everything else. Still, it's like what I'm remembering happened only yesterday. First, the volunteer fire department held a celebratory parade. They went down Main Street carrying lighted torches. A marching band played, but in some other city, maybe Belgrade or Zagreb. Which made it no less celebratory. And from the third floor of the DEPARTMENT STORE, flashing in the tittering lights, thick clouds of small tinfoil hammers and sickles were falling.

All decked out, in the center of the ground floor, the Director was standing and greeting the esteemed invitees. All around, on the ground, there was an incredible crowd moving around, of robot toys, monkeys with cymbals, tanks, jeeps and trucks—the latest word in Soviet technology. Somebody brought me there, too. That's the only way I can explain how I saw there in the crowd, just for an instant of course, the face of the little girl about whom, much later, I wanted to write a novel.

That is the memory I'm talking about. About the opening of a department store. Department stores are a thing of the past for me. What was that angelic face doing in Bajina Bašta? I asked myself that question for years. And why did she leave so quickly (and so permanently) my life, if one can call IT that. Ultimately, the very thought of Margaux— that's what I called her—always brought a ray of sunshine into the endless dreariness of my days.

At that moment, I saw Luke the priest. He was just then exiting the Evropa tavern, walking straight through the wall. I wanted to be bewildered but changed my mind. The world is falling apart. There's nothing strange about someone walking straight through a wall. Anyone can do it, but out of habit no one even tries. And, at the end of the day, what good would it do?

The Mongolian Travel Guide

Bügd Nayramadakh Mongol Ard Uls—the People's Republic of Mongolia, 1,565,000 square kilometers, population 1,710,000. A remote country in central Asia, inhabited by the descendants of Genghis Khan, apparitions, and an occasional European settler. Bordered by the PR of China and the USSR. No matter where a person is here, it's only a day's walk to *nowhere*.

What am I doing in Mongolia, I asked myself instead of the customs officer, who asked me the very same thing. Formally, I had come to write a Baedeker, a special report sponsored by *Epoch* magazine, whose first issue will appear in a few years. If they find someone to found it and if money is provided for it, which I doubt. Just as I doubt everything else. But a job is a job. That's what professional ethics demand. Finally, I was obligated to do so by my deceased friend, and besides, the place was far enough from the shitty one where I lived. And what about it? I arrived in Ulaanbaatar and established that it also was a shitty, truly remote place. It was the most far-removed package at the Globtour Agency. The clerk hardly found the brochure in the far east of the agency. But that's the way the world is: perhaps it's even better that way, because, as Luther said, "there where it's better—there it's twice as bad."

The place, as I was saying, was as shitty as any other, and in every last one of them there are plenty of bums and idiots ready to talk for hours about the origins, history, and views of their city; to compile facts, names, years, and centuries, just to ensure themselves ontological justification, continuity, and vindication for the fact that they live in such a pit. Only Japanese tourists fall for it. They click away with their Nikons, taking pictures of chickens in the muddy streets, pictures of beggars, besmirched children, wrinkly old women, groups of drunk young men . . . The rare Western oddballs who live here are actually hiding from ontology, knowing that everything here is just a carefully directed production for foreigners; they wave their hands in disgust and wander into a hotel lobby to drown their sorrows in drink.

At the entrance to the airport building, I was met by two officials with a yellow armband. I didn't know what to do with the yellow armband. However, there is a decree from the Ministry of Information of the PR of Mongolia, according to which all foreign correspondents must wear a yellow armband with the Star of David on the right sleeve of their overcoats. That decree caused a storm of protest from the so-called progressive movement across the world. What else could you expect from feminists, liberals, and ignoramuses? Quite quickly, I discovered that every similarity between that decree and the Nazis' was accidental. Yellow is, in fact, the color of the Mongolian race, and the six sides of the star are symbols of the heavenly lotus—that is, of the six virtues that are supposed to characterize men of letters unless they want to be born as rhinoceroses in the next incarnation. The basis of it is actually a hexagram, the most commonplace, journalistic mandala. The Ministry of Information ultimately published a statement that cleared up the misunderstanding, and the Star of David was replaced with PRESS, in Cyrillic letters: ПРЕСС. The liberals, feminists, the Green Party, and even the Belgrade communists simply refused to be satisfied. Again protests. The communists, of course (the avant-garde), were at the forefront. The Municipal Committee organized spontaneous demonstrations, and groups of secret police, students, and ne'er-do-wells headed for the Mongolian embassy. The Mongolian government reacted immediately: instead of yellow armbands, they introduced red ones that said RENMIN. In the meantime, interest in the affair about correspondents' armbands began to wane, because on the beach of Lloret de Mar two dead dolphins were found, so the protestors quit searching for the Mongolian embassy and headed for the Spanish one. It all ended peacefully, but the nasty, undeserved shadow of anti-Semitism fell on the people of Mongolia. But, every evil thing brings about something good as well. The oil-producing countries, all Arab, lowered the price by an entire fourteen dollars per barrel for the Mongolian refineries. No one was especially thrilled by that; anyway, gas in Mongolia is sold for almost nothing, and most of the population uses horses as their means of transportation.

One more note of interest: the morning when I arrived in Ulaanbaatar, they executed the on-duty meteorologist by firing squad. The preceding day, he'd forecast sunny and windy weather and snow flurries fell the next morning. The judge had no mercy. Tsedenbal didn't want to sign a stay. Cruel! Perhaps. But that's the way it is in real socialism. In Yugoslavia after the war, didn't they execute people just for having a house and a little money? Ultimately, that's sovereign Mongolia's internal affair. But there's one more thing to say here: in the Middle East, meteorology is one of the most respected professions. At the colleges, they only take in the best candidates selected from the multitude who apply—the ones with impeccable pasts. The studies, because of the exceptionally unstable and unpredictable climate, last all of fifteen years. During that time, students study the ancient learning of India and China together with the most modern achievements of Western science. So much concern over meteorology has gradually led to a state of affairs in which weather conditions don't depend on monsoons, cyclones, and anti-cyclones, but on the long-term forecast of the Central Committee of the

Meteorological Service. Nothing here is left to chance. But again, meteorologists must guess whether it will rain or if the sun will shine. Through the coordinated work of teams of scientists, through unprecedented discipline and constant observation, they've reached the point where rivers change their courses according to need and the foreseen annual amount of rainfall is equally distributed all over the territory. So now, if someone makes a mistake, even with such organizational resources—it's off with his head. No one is particularly upset about that. Oriental fatalism! For them, in keeping with the teaching of Buddhist monks, the homeland is just a camp in the desert. And human life—that's just an incidental agglomeration of the extra-temporal particles of nothingness.

The Buddhist tradition is the reason for the spectacular success of communist doctrine in Mongolia. There are so many points of contact: the rejection of gods, disrepair and a lack of interest in things of this world, disdain toward democratic recklessness. It's hard to bring such a claim into accord with my own religiosity, which might also be just a simulation. I will not refer to Aristotle or Thomas Aquinas. Certainly not. Totalitarianism and religiosity are not at odds. The subjects of tyrannical regimes should be infinitely grateful to Providence that it has authorized them to put up with the multitude of difficulties under totalitarianism. That's a sign of God's special favor. Because if people don't want to fast, to suffer, to be humiliated, to curse the moment they were born—in that case they are certainly bound for hell. If the Son of God had to be crucified, the mere mortal must be thoroughly thrashed in the cellar of some sort of security service, if he wants eternal life. And he does. Everyone does. It's just that today, at the turn of the twenty-first century, no one wants to suffer, at least not voluntarily; everyone wants yachts, the high life, piles of money and luxury. *Contradictio in adiecto!* And that's why God put the ones he intends to save in one of the totalitarian states. If not by grace, then by force, or, as that lovely Latin proverb states: fortune leads the wise and drags along the stupid. And thus the heavenly chosen scuffle in lines outside of half-empty stores, shivering in clammy dens, putting up with humiliation and preferring to remain silent. No, no one can convince me that this is bad. All these countries remind me of huge monasteries where the monks—the citizens—do penance for the sins of the world. In the end, Mongolia is not even the vanguard of strictness. In Burkina Faso, for example, you can end up on the gallows for poor spelling.

One of the little-known tourist attractions of Mongolia is the border where dreams and waking permeate each other. Once again, because of a decree by the Ministry of Education, this attraction is reluctantly mentioned, and rarely is anyone interested in it. I had an opportunity to encounter this phenomenon. Tramping through the mud from the airport (by decree of the Ministry of Transportation, which can be reduced more or less to this: since you already flew thousands of kilometers, it's only right that you walk the last fifteen or so); as I was saying—tramping through the mud, I ran into a Protestant bishop from Holland, who'd just noticed a strange sight: me, muddy up to my waist, loaded down with two suitcases. His pupils dilated in wonderment. I looked at my watch, did the calculations, in Amsterdam it was one in the morning; the bishop was dreaming in his bed without a care in the world. This was the last drop in the cup of strange dreams which, rather bitterly, the bishop had been drinking all night. He jerked up out of his sleep, but too quickly; his soul did not manage to return to him in Amsterdam along the astral plane, so he woke up right next to me, in Ulaanbaatar, barefoot and in his nightshirt. He most probably would have lost his mind, perhaps he would have dispersed like mist, if I hadn't explained some of the particulars of this place in time. In fact, I might have made everything up, led along by my Christian solidarity. With a clear conscience. The differences between documentary and fictional materials are purely formal, with the proviso that the fictional are often favored because they are more convincing and certainly closer to the truth. That was what saved the misfortunate bishop. We headed off, looking like vagabonds, toward the Dutch embassy. Like hell we did. Holland and Mongolia do not have diplomatic relations. All right then, let's look for the Belgian embassy, which represents Dutch interests. We were received by the first secretary of the embassy, who

gave it some thought and then made his decision: the
bishop would be issued a passport and a permit to work
as a missionary; he was to stay—the secretary said—
two to three years in Ulaanbaatar, while the metaphysical scandal was dealt with, and then he could go home.
The bishop agreed. And he even added that it was his
lifelong dream to become a missionary in some remote
country. There, you see, sometimes dreams do come
true. As we will hear—he was fairly successful in his
missionary work. He built a rather small church in the
suburbs of Ulaanbaatar, gathered a devoted flock, and
even translated the works of Paul Tillich and Søren
Kierkegaard into Mongolian. Then he got down to work
on a translation of Luther's *Bible*. Since we're talking
about literature, I was filled with pride when I found
out that there was a fairly large number of translations
of Yugoslav authors in Ulaanbaatar's bookshops. Here
is a partial listing: Dobrica Ćosić, *The Eagles Fly Early*;
Antonije Isaković, *The Red Scarf and Other Stories*; Josip
Broz Tito, *Collected Works*; Franjo Tuđman, *Horrors of
War: Historical Reality and Philosophy*. Let's not dig too
deep into the translators' choices. It's important that the
books get translated. And that the translations sound
very poetic. Like the title of Ćosić's book, *The Eagles Fly
Early*, which is *Artachumn mingolcan*, if memory serves
me correctly.

The Russians are a story unto themselves. Advisers,
officers, instructors, engineers, their wives and children,
are all KGB agents. They all live at the Ulaanbaatar

Hotel and do their shopping at a mall surrounded by high walls with barbed wire on top. The Russians just can't get by without walls and barbed wire, nothing can be changed about that. Otherwise, they're absolutely fine. Open-hearted Slavic souls. Since their country is nowhere to be found (or is found everywhere), they feel at home no matter where they are. All the live-long day and all through the night, balalaikas and accordions can be heard playing at the hotel . . . Versions of "Kalinka" and "Rabinushka" echo out, celebratory gunfire clatters from Kalashnikovs. At the anniversaries of the Great October Revolution, they fire off a couple of surface-to-surface missiles and the projectiles explode with great style in the hills outside of Ulaanbaatar. Since Dostoyevsky's spirit has become an essential component of their genetic code, occasionally it happens that a conscientious major of some sort, in a fit of unexpected enlightenment, rips off his uniform (highly decorated and beautiful) and becomes a Buddhist monk. Not long afterward, the former major becomes the head lama and immediately fences the temple off with barbed wire. However, the average lifespan of a deserter from the Red Army is hardly ever longer than two or three years. Four at the most. And they rarely die from natural causes. That's just the way it is: *per aspera ad astra*.

Mongolian economic policy. That's also a story unto itself. I'm no expert in economy; economy nauseates me and thus I'm leaving my ramblings on that topic out of the final text of my article. Essentially, the Mongolian model, like everything else in the Far East, is quite simple. The stores are well supplied. And the prices? Everything, literally everything, from a needle to a locomotive, calculated in German Marks costs exactly five marks. With my own eyes I saw the latest BMW model for that price. But, that's also how much a box of matches costs. Or a postage stamp. Crowds of shoppers nowhere to be found, no maddened consumers caught up in the fever, no advertisements or disloyal competition anywhere. With an average paycheck, a citizen can buy up to twenty automobiles. Yes, but one should also buy a sack of rice or two, some butter, tea, a few cigarettes. Such a policy stimulates saving. It would be impossible, for example, to see children whiling away the day in front of a building, striking matches. In Ulaanbaatar, a match is a sacred object. Zero point inflation, annual production growth 0.2%, unemployment zero. For centuries already. And always the same. That's the secret of the ever-present natural radiance of the Mongols' faces and of their internal strength, which, under Genghis Khan, conquered the then extant world in the course of a few weeks. In no time flat. The wise riders of the steppes quickly realized that there's nothing worthwhile in the West. As they came—so they left. Packed up their yurts, mounted their steeds, and went back to their plateau.

Since we're talking about prices, the satisfaction of visiting one of the local brothels also costs five euros.

Indeed, five euros in Mongolia is a small fortune, but I told myself: enough now! In book after book you write about ostensibly edifying topics, and there is nothing edifying about you. On the contrary. Come on: establish a precedent, get drunk, visit a whorehouse, hit life's bottom, roll in the mud so that later you'll have more to regret. So I did. Nothing easier than finding a house of ill repute in Ulaanbaatar. You just look for one of the many fishmongers, go in disinterestedly, and hop on one leg to the door for "personnel only." The rest is simple. The madam leads you into sweet-smelling rooms. One might ask: why are there bordellos in Ulaanbaatar? Naive bastard. Even in the western part of Europe, there there's a predominant misconception that there are no whorehouses in communist countries. Wrong right from the start. There are, in all of them. Or better said: there are, and there aren't. For foreigners they exist, for the locals they don't. That's not because of the concern for the health and morale of the local population—communists and their morale—but because the communist potentates do not allow their subjects any sort of satisfaction; they force them to masturbate, to slam their heads into walls, to rape, to have their spines dry up, to suffer from pubescent madness, because it's easiest to manipulate imbeciles and frustrated people. Back home, let's say, in Yugoslavia, those hidden houses of ill repute are located in tire shops. Basically, it's important that there's something hanging in front of the building, the way there's a red light in civilized countries. In

Yugoslavia, the secret sign for entering looks like this: the visitor goes into the tire shop, holding his left ear in his right hand and singing the Marseillaise. The repairman points at a door at the back of the workshop, and the rest is as easy as pie. As for Russia, China, and Korea—how things are done there—I don't know. We should ask around.

As I was saying, I hopped into the fishmonger's, found the personnel door, and out came a eunuch with a cup of tea and a warm welcome. There was plenty for me to see: in the middle of the room, surrounded by beauties, was my acquaintance, Bishop Van den Garten. To be respectful, I pretended that the bishop was there in his role as a missionary. Anyway, I had no evidence to the contrary: all of them were fully clothed. But that didn't necessarily mean anything; Eastern sexual techniques are countless and indescribable. The bishop immediately came up to me and offered me a cup of tea. We sat down. "My son," he started circumspectly, "have you lost your faith?" I thought about it for a while. I drank the second cup of tea as well, and then ordered a whisky so that they'd stop offering me that swill. "In order for a man to believe," I said, "he has to be dead—far from this world." The bishop grew serious. He asked why I said that. "That's only true under ideal circumstances," I tried to explain. "Actually, I haven't lost my faith, but I'm acting like I have. Ultimately, I think that you Protestants (nothing personal) are formulating things incorrectly. We Orthodox folk look at it a little differently. We wonder: has God lost his faith in me, has he grown tired of my nonsense, my endless repetition of sins, and my cowardly prayers asking forgiveness. Likewise, I think that God, in principle, never abandons anyone for good; he simply shoves them into a corner." The priest was silent for a while. Then he said, "I, unfortunately, have lost my faith. That's why I'm being so cruelly punished. You see, I no longer believe in God, and I can't be a sinner. Do you understand the situation I'm in?" "Yes and no," I said. "What is it you really want? You lack the patience to withstand temptations. You think you can get to heaven on an express train from the armchair in your office in Amsterdam. You have to suffer a little bit. And stop pissing me off, or otherwise I'll kill you like a dog." "But that's a sin!" the bishop shouted. Well, depends on how you look at it. There's a papal bull from 1678, according to which murdering a Protestant bishop is a godly act. Consequently, I could have killed the bishop, proselyted to Catholicism, received forgiveness, and gone back to Orthodoxy. But that just wasn't like me. Not because I was too righteous to kill a man, but because I was too lazy to fiddle with all that unavoidable theological–administrative malarkey. Naturally, this was all just scholastic speculation. Then, the guy running the whore house got involved in our conversation. "You know," he said, "you are respectable guests, but this is not a school of theology, but a bordello. Out of respect for one of our most valued clients—the Belgian ambassador who is Mr. Van den Garten's sponsor—I allow him to spread the truths of his religion here twice a month, but it's not good to overdo things." The bishop apologized and left. A fishtail was peeping out of his coat pocket. As camouflage, I suppose. But I remained, confronted with a delicate assignment: a description of the idiosyncrasies of Mongolian sexuality.

Still, nothing came of that. The girl I chose, as soon as we got behind the curtain, fell on her knees and began to beg me in broken Russian. "Sir, I just heard you talking with the bishop and, although I didn't understand a single word, I did get that you're a Christian. You see, I've converted to Christianity. You'll understand, then, that it's horribly unpleasant for me to be involved in debauchery." What other choice did I have but to understand her? Could I have dared to insist on my whorehouse rights, and then, one day, when I stand before the Last Judgment, not hear the condemnation? "All of it, all of it, and the uncountable committed sins and the lengthy list of drinking binges, blasphemies, and the hardness of heart! But did you really have to travel twelve thousand miles just to force one poor converted soul into sin." "It's all right," I said to her, "consider it done." Either way, I went into the brothel led more by curiosity than by lust. And besides, the girl was ugly. Very happy, my not-meant-to-be lover started making another pot of disgusting Mongolian tea. I was disheartened: I had just done a good deed, and here I was lying: I said that I went there out of curiosity and not lust. But even that is, after all, a kind of improvement: possible future readers won't have a chance to spice up their lives with lascivious details. Better if they buy pulp fiction, sex magazines, and thus, indirectly, help the regime to survive, the same regime that's leading them to destruction. After all (later I'd tell the girl this), I had sworn that all my books would speak of horrors, in a comic way if possible. Because there are only two things in the world: humor and horror. The girl just didn't get it. I attempted to explain it to her. "For example," I said, "Mongolian tea is awful, but the way you prepare it is cute and humorous; namely, as you warm the water you stand on your heads, and before adding the tea leaves, butter, and salt, you do a flip and sing a few bars of the ancient 'Ode to Tea' from the sixth century." She understood nothing. So, I said good-bye and hit the road. Like hell I did. The fishmonger wouldn't allow me to leave. "Your fish, your fish!" he kept rabidly shouting. Ah, the customs of faraway exotic countries. I bought my five and a half kilograms, paid my five marks and went out into the street feeling like the ultimate idiot, and I didn't dare to simply throw the fish into a garbage can because article 67 of the Criminal Code of the PR of Mongolia strictly forbids throwing food away. The punishment is five to fifteen years of high-security prison.

And when a day starts off poorly, it finishes even worse. Entering the hotel lobby, I was exposed to the discreet smirks of the personnel and the live-in guests: everyone knew that I'd been to the bordello—and that

I'd proved to be a wimp. I sat at the bar and ordered a double whiskey in order to steep my sadness, shame, and melancholy in alcohol. And then—I almost fell off the barstool: some forty feet from me, leaning back in a leather armchair, Charlotte Rampling was sitting, drinking cappuccino, and leafing through *Time* magazine. I rubbed my eyes. This was not my dreamed-up priest from Amsterdam; it really was Charlotte Rampling, the heroine of a film I used to love: *The Night Porter*.

The whole business about Miss Rampling was explained to me by the doyen of the correspondents, a guy named Chuck, writer for the long-since out-of-print *Boston Evening News*. He said that Miss Rampling spends eight months out of the year in Mongolia. She leaves, makes a movie, gets paid, and comes back. She speaks with no one. She reads the papers and drinks cappuccino. We drank long and hard that night, Chuck and I. Like me, he was also a citizen of alcoholism, the best means of escaping one's homeland, political systems, TV networks, and all the creeps who gather around such nonsense. Chuck's Life Story went something like this: he was born in a small town in Missouri as the son of a well-off farmer. He was an exemplary child, a good student, he sang the American National Anthem, hated blacks and communists, went to one of the countless churches on Sunday; he never stole or lied, nor did he ever masturbate. He helped the elderly and the blind cross the street. And then came the turnabout: he met an old Native American witch doctor, who introduced him to the secrets of pre-Columbian magic. The spells and rituals opened his eyes. He realized that the American Way of Life is just a nasty deception, and that every inhabitant of the USA has exactly 237 evil demons, as opposed to Europe, where the per capita number is just twelve, except for Russia, Romania, Bulgaria, and Yugoslavia, where there are practically no devils because their work in those countries is already done. Just one on guard here and there, visiting the deserted cities and enticing into evil those rare people who haven't yet succumbed to the collective obsession. Pedantically, as only an American can, he classified these facts and began publishing a series of articles. This was during the McCarthy witch hunts. They accused him of being a communist. So he became one. That's how powerful public opinion is in America. Formerly an excellent student, formerly an Indian witch doctor, he registered with the Communist Party of America. Only then did he get really sick of his life, and so started drinking.

"An excellent disinfectant," he told me: "only alcohol can wash away all the nonsense clogging your brain. There are better means, but they're lethal. And you should know, if you see a guy who doesn't drink, stay a hundred miles from him. A person who can put up with all the misery of this world, without the use of drugs or alcohol, surely does not have a soul."

Yeah, then the liberals, the progressive public (and one should know that back then they weren't such enormous idiots as they are today), stepped onto the scene, and they took up Chuck's cause. He got a job at the abovementioned newspaper and was quickly thereafter appointed to be their correspondent in Ulaanbaatar. Soon after, the newspaper quit being published, and Chuck remained in Mongolia. Out of inertia. Nobody bothered him. Nobody asked him to extend his visa. Nobody sent him hotel bills. Thanks to the Security Services. It's a strictly kept secret (and undeniable fact) that the members of those services are notorious drunks, and drunks have compassion for one another. Anyway, Chuck made a reasonable living; he gave English classes to children from the better homes in Ulaanbaatar. I believe he obtained citizenship as well. And he didn't want to go anywhere. He was completely right about that. I've already said that all places are equally shitty and nonsensical, and the profits of traveling are only earned by tourist agencies. People travel in search of excitement, beauty, and . . . Who am I kidding? They travel looking for the Devil, and they usually find him.

My life story was different from the outset. Pure bullshit. I have neither mother nor father. I have no one. God created me out of nothing (just like everything else) so that I could finish up some of the meaningless jobs resulting from Providence. Nothing special. On September 6 one year, I simply showed up in the first grade of elementary school. Books, notebooks, pencil case—everything was in its place. However, because of that I didn't have any sort of complex, especially no Freudian ones. I already knew *Hamlet* by heart.

All that's a lot of blabbering. Both the complexes and
Hamlet. There is no such person, who has a complex,
who has anything except metabolic processes, and the
traumas, the complexes, and the stress—that's all just
an exaggeration meant to attribute a certain amount of
importance to the self. Strictly speaking, no one even
has a biography; all of that has been written, defined,
calculated by others. Individual human freedom comes
down to a choice: to smoke, or not to smoke; to drink
or not to drink. Life stories! That's a way to trick the
Lord God. A nonsensical one, of course. Because God
actually brings people into the world so that they can see
that the world is a shitty place and come running back
to His embrace as quickly as possible. Like hell! Man is a
strange creature. This or that catches his fancy; suddenly,
he refuses to die, and since he knows deep down that he's
not playing by the Rules of the Game, he starts telling
lies about how things supposedly happened. Reasons,
reasons, reasons. My mission, for example, is to trash
the world and people, to humiliate myself and others,
to contradict everything and everyone. Unfortunately,
I'm not doing a very good job. If I had, incidentally,
been sent into the world by the Mafia, I would have
long since have been decomposing at the bottom of one
of the New York harbors, my feet encased in two hundred pounds of cement. I'd like to run away from my
responsibilities (Jonas wanted to do the same), to drive
an expensive car, to cruise on a yacht, surrounded by
beauties and snorting cocaine. Namely, in addition to

God's providence, there is also the Devil's: the one that leads people to ruin themselves happily and completely. However, thanks to God's providence, His persistence in setting me on the right path, I never even met my first love—so I loved her absolutely platonically and I never wrote that book of ten thousand pages in which I describe her departure. In truth, God was beneficent; He allowed me to see her once, briefly, when they opened the department store in Bajina Bašta. That's also why I started drinking. Because she was always within reach, because I always felt her presence, because I recognized her in some detail on the face of every pretty passerby (the differences between women are negligible anyway). I felt her absence. For days, months, years. So did she, I think. The same way other people in love in this world feel *presence*, we felt *absence*. Whenever the confluence of circumstances threatened to set things up so that our meeting was unavoidable, God's finger would intervene, so my undestined Diotima would get, let's say, a call from her uncle in Cleveland announcing his visit. Or she'd meet some handsome fellow. Or she'd get hit by a car. Or something or other. And because of that we both felt a terrible emptiness in our souls; I, in truth, had it incomparably worse because, in accord with the doctrine of Charles the Hideous—women hardly have a soul, and that soul is inverted, vaginal one might say, so that she experienced that sadness of separation from her animus as premenstrual pains. I flatter myself that they were exceptionally strong, those pains. But that's why Midol exists. Perhaps that's actually the reason I headed for Ulaanbaatar in the first place. Either to find her in some impossible place, or to hide from her. I don't know. I think, actually, even if we'd ever met, I'd still feel this terrible emptiness in my soul. That's simply my fate. My cross to bear. And perhaps my salvation.

But, as I said, my life story and Chuck's occasionally met in alcohol, floating like two fetuses in a jar of formaldehyde. Nothing new in that. People always come together in order to indulge in vices and mortal sins. However, unlike Chuck, who was full of booze and American confidence, I always got roles to play. Let's consider this one, for example: the poet. I played it for a good ten years or so, with a hefty amount of bitterness, because it was so utterly episodic. Basically, I was supposed to wear a shirt with purple and black stripes, black bell-bottoms, to act like an idiot, here and there to scribble out a line or two, and to drink, which was my only comfort. Yet when I remember that my previous— my first—role (from which sprang the proto-biographical and mythological era of my life so-called) was that of an athlete, then this one doesn't seem so bad after all. Yeah, all those kilometers run at a sprint, all those goals scored against me, which only added to my feeling of absolute failure. It wasn't so bad being a poet. And in between the roles (no longer than a few months), they let me rest. No feelings of guilt, or disgust . . . I really did enjoy myself . . .

To toast to that, Chuck and I drank one more glass

and called the coolies to carry us to our rooms. Outside my room, a Mongolian wrestler was standing at attention, in traditional garb, with a rifle over his shoulder, all oiled up; in Ulaanbaatar, these are the messengers. He handed me a letter and rushed off like the wind. And in the letter? The papal nuncio to the government of the PR of Mongolia, Monsignor Benedetti, wrote:

> Dear Sir,
> We have been told that today, in a place not worthy of mention, you threatened the Protestant bishop Van den Garten with a nonexistent bull of the Holy Father, and thus insulted the Holy See. The fact that Bishop Van den Garten is just a dream is no excuse for such an unacceptable act. If such a thing were to repeat itself, I am putting you on notice that the reach of the Curia is long and merciless. Should you insult the Vatican once more, we will proselytize you from Orthodoxy into the Catholic faith and burn you as a heretic.

The Vatican-Comintern conspiracy, it seems, is ongoing. Ad infinitum.

What was I saying: why did I come to Mongolia? To write a travel guide. Nonsense. Let's say, I came here in order to try once again to find something out about myself. I don't know who I am. I never have. I did not, like most people, fall into the trap of names and other stupidities the government gives you as soon as you move from the status of specter to the status of mannequin. We already mentioned it: everyone gets their roles, and I—since I wasn't very promising—was given the most peripheral ones. Basara, that's just a storefront. Just as it says "Barber Shop" outside the hairdresser's, BASARA is written on the covers of my books, and I even have to pay taxes because of that. Then again, although I don't know who's sitting inside the dark literary store with the abovementioned storefront, many things are clear to me, and that's where my Golgotha begins. How can one embrace clarity and introduce it into the den of language which mostly serves for lying, tattling, and giving false testimony . . . Language that I simultaneously fear and loathe. There is no doubt that, had I been born in the eleventh or twelfth century, I'd be a mystic. I'd remain silent and thus search for serenity. But I was born way too late. And that's why I never hurry, though that doesn't mean that I'm relaxed. On the contrary! I'm constantly tense and worried by the maniacal and worthless era of the twentieth century. I don't believe in anything except God. But God is unreachable. Absent, but still terrifying. Maybe that's actually why Providence didn't allow me to meet my one and only love. So that I would learn that distance and absence only amplify one's desire for a beloved.

Pff, those are all just descriptions of the deepest layers of my personality, which I have reached in the archeological excavations of the soul that belongs to it. I remained silent about the few golden particles found in the thick layers of sludge. God tossed them to me as if I were a dog, which essentially I am, in order to comfort me even though I don't deserve it. Just so there's no confusion, why it is that I'm basically a dog: I wander about aimlessly, I'm flea-infested but still I'm faithful. Faithful! That's an exaggeration. More likely I'm a hyena. Otherwise, on the outside I'm a man like any other. Even worse because of the abovementioned diluvial layers of my psyche, I'm somehow more hollow than other people. But it remains the case that inside always means something else, I say it's so, and I'll continue to say so regardless of the danger that I'll be exposed to the indignation of the feminists, leftists, liberals, and a myriad of Belgrade mayors. I've known a whole series of people who are, on the inside—just as I am a hyena—foxes, falcons, crows, bulldogs, soccer balls, aquariums, or some such stuff. By chance, I began to write because, in my youth, when I was still unspoiled, I looked a bit like an inkstand and quill. It will never be clear to me why I started writing. It certainly wasn't out of ambition. Never, except in my boyhood fantasies when I wanted to be a cosmonaut, did I ever have any kind of ambition. I wasn't really longing for a career. I just wanted everyone to leave me alone, simply to go on living without a plan. Like hell! This world is awful indeed, because no one ever leaves anyone alone, because deep down in our souls we're all tyrants and reformers, to put it simply: because each of us has the wild idea that the entire universe—no more, no less—should be ordered in accordance with our beliefs and needs. It's just a matter of ability and the hand of fate as to how great the amount of evil will be heaped on the surroundings by this or that person. That's why I never felt any sort of hatred, disdain, or disgust toward the biggest bad guys in history. Nero, Caligula, Hitler, Stalin—they're all just you or me placed under a microscope, magnified several thousand times. Objectively speaking: the meaningless creatures around us inflict us with greater evil. Who ever did Hitler give a slap to, inform on them to the police? The giants of evil didn't subjugate us. We were the ones who created them, raised them up from mediocrity, and placed them on the throne—just so we could dump all our guilt on their backs.

But that's not the reason I started writing either. Everything just stated was only a reflection from the period after I started writing. Here I'm interested in that *I* from the period before that. Was it confiscated? Requisitioned? Whatever the case, that fellow wasn't very interested in literature. Almost not at all. To be totally honest: not at all. I was interested in languages, but I was always too lazy to learn them. So—my fate. Or by order of the Central Committee? Back then everything was planned. Or the strange affinity I had for paranoia, which, if I'd only had the luck, would have sent me into madness, and from there into the maternal security of an insane asylum—insane asylums are the rare remaining places where the soul is ever even mentioned. I never got free of my paranoia. That's actually how I survived. Here, let's take an example: as soon as someone begins to praise advancement—the advantages of, say, electricity—I immediately think to myself: they didn't discover electricity in order to offer its conveniences to the wider masses, but in order to create the electric chair. Then again I'm not disappointed. How can it be explained? Why explain it?

My company in Ulaanbaatar was slowly expanding; into the borders of our literary Bantustan came pouring an ever greater number of more or less fictional subjects. In addition to Chuck and the ubiquitous Bishop Van den Garten (who relentlessly insisted that the article *den* should be written *der*), Lama Vladimir Tikhonov (one of the Soviet converts), and a certain Mr. Mercier. That's the old scoundrel who, for a hefty sum, introduced Sylvia Kristel into the finesses of oriental sin in the movie *Emmanuelle*. The fellow in fact had been dead for five years already, but no one minds that in Mongolia, where people are ultimately polite even toward those who are quite obviously corpses, which Mr. Mercier certainly wasn't. He was a tough old bird, that Mercier, as if he'd come from the pen of the degenerate Marquis de Sade. For understandable reasons, he couldn't have sexual relationships, but he didn't stink too much. He was still wearing that white suit from the film, and that made the Mongols feel sorry for him, because in the East white is the color of mourning. Everyone thought that he'd lost a loved one, which was in some ways true: he had died. Lama, what else, Tikhonov, on his orange monk's robes, wore the gilded epaulettes of a colonel of the Red Army and the Order of Lenin. Although he'd accepted Buddhism wholeheartedly, as only a Russian can, he was still working for the KGB and he could simply not give some things up: brocade, lampas, epaulettes, and vodka. Vodka—that's what drew him closer to us. Then from somewhere Dr. Andreotti showed up, Jung's former student. Every afternoon, until late into the night, we met in the lobby of the Genghis Khan Hotel. Lama Tikhonov would mumble out *Mahasatti—patanasuttam* to chase out the evil spirits and then we began to talk as if we were windup dolls. Like in *One Thousand and One Nights.* Except that in our case, every evening Scheherazade was a different person, and no one was Shahryar. Out of respect for the social order of the PR of Mongolia.

One night, when we were already deep in our cups, Mr. Mercier interrupted the silence with his graveyard voice.

"I was, gentlemen, not afraid to die when my time came. No, not at all. However, I had made a fairly serious amount of money, I had no heirs, so I said to myself: why not just fritter it all away? That's actually why I came to Mongolia, a cold and windy country, where I can waste away the rest of my days. And so that later it would be less unpleasant in hell for me. Because, I must mention, in these circumstances my body temperature is always the same as the surrounding temperature. Because of entropy. There were days when it was down to thirty degrees below zero. An awful feeling. I'm not sorry about anything, but I think I wasted my life. But, in return, I know a lot of things that only the dead know, because in a certain sense I have dual citizenship."

"What things are those?" Van den Garten inquired.

"Well, for example, I know that all people are not the same. I don't mean the psychological and morphological differences, but the ontological ones. Or, better said—the temporal differences."

"It's really hard to believe that!" Van den Garten retorted.

"That's true," Mercier went on, "but it's hard to believe in anything except food, drink, sex, hard work, and the rest of the poppycock. But dead men don't lie. They cannot. That's a privilege of the living. I'm telling you that there are three kinds of people in history: those whose internal time runs faster than the external; those whose internal time is synchronic with the external; and those whose internal time is slower than the external. Those are the rarest."

Here, he paused.

"Would you like for me to tell you about that?"

At the moment when he pronounced the question, somewhere between the last vibrations of his voice and the loud approval of the others, I experienced a sort of trivial enlightenment. Perhaps this trip to the East was not so meaningless. "It seems that this corpse is right," I thought in that instant, connecting his theory with the constant slipping away of that girl, my Anima, the one about whom I wished to write a novel of ten thousand pages. I was overcome with a sadness at the thought of the fees for such a thick tome, which I'll never write. This wasn't, after all, a question of the Vatican-Comintern conspiracy but just the order of the world and humankind. Simply, our internal temporal flows did not overlap, and no force in the world could have arranged for us to meet.

Mr. Mercier began to talk . . .

The Tractate of the Late Mr. Mercier on the Three Kinds of Internal Time

GENTLEMEN, THE SCHOLARSHIP I am about to present you here in its pitiful remains is nothing new. Like most worthwhile disciplines, it has been forgotten and left to the intellectual curiosity of the dead. As early as the fourth century, one imaginary author wrote about two kinds of time: about external and internal time. Since I am new to the otherworld, I haven't had time to study that manuscript in detail. But briefly, it says that real time is internal, individual, and that external time is dependent on it, its double after a fashion. When the world used to be somehow hierarchically ordered, those two times coexisted in relative harmony. That is what the modern hacks call "The Golden Age." That's why those fabulous old-ages which are mentioned in the Old Testament are actually not exaggerations; those are facts. Ephemerality did not just slip into our world accidentally. On one occasion my friend, the Hungarian writer and wine connoisseur Béla Hamvas, narrated to me how this temporal debacle came about.

"Up until about six hundred years before the modern era," Hamvas said, "human history was simply all related; and then, over one or two generations, but certainly not more than three, time changed. The eras that came before and after that six hundredth year are separated by an intangible curtain; what is in front of the curtain is found here with us, and it's clear; whatever is behind the curtain has to be guessed at. Human personalities suddenly changed into the improbable entities. The contours of events were erased. Being became incomprehensible. About Confucius, we have detailed facts that reach all the way into his private life; the personhood of Lao-Tse, only a generation older, is lost in darkness. About Heraclitus we have many of the important facts; the being of Pythagoras, who was only a few years older than him, is a legend. Man so lost the ground under his feet that he believes that he's not walking on earth but upon some unknown constellation. Elementary things became uncertain; events and personalities became ungraspable; being is enigmatic, and time is a blur."[3]

Hamvas explained to me that it happened because

---

3 Related to this, the opinion of one other author (X. Paldum) should be mentioned, stating that the end of history will be analogous to the beginning of it. That is, from the historical period, gradually we will move into the mythical one, and the leadership in events will consist of pseudo-mythological characters, people without an ontological foundation or identity; events will not be clear, and consequences will come before causes. (Author's note)

people became opaque. Because they closed up inside themselves. In the terms of physics: they lost contact with the external world and became closed systems which, as is well known, very quickly fail because of entropy. So now, external time, left to its own devices, has become an uncontrolled randomness without continuity: sometimes it rushes past like a hurricane, sometimes it just drags along, every once in a while it stops completely. In order to gain control, people constructed timepieces; thus, they created the illusion of time. But that's just fiddling with space, in fact. Timepieces, beginning with water clocks and sundials, and all the way down to atomic clocks, are nothing more than an illusion. And that's why everything in time is an illusion. Now it's become clear that absurdities and nihilism are the most rational viewpoints in the world, if this mess in which we eke out our days can even be called that anymore. In some way, nihilism is a form of religiousness in this time. Nothing can be known anymore. It certainly is not to be ruled out that we have long been in hell, but that, like Melanchthon, we have overlooked that fact.

"But," the bishop attempted to object, "that is in conflict with the fundamental teachings of Christianity."

"Certainly," held Mr. Mercier, "only that doesn't mean that the teachings of Christianity aren't true. God is doing his job and saving those he intends to. I wanted to say that the holy books are falsified like all the others. The lie has not just taken control of the world—it has become ontologized; it has become the very *esse* of our miserable existence. Everyone lies. No longer out of self-interest or an excess of fantasy. People lie because they're convinced that they're telling the truth. But the lie has only one goal: to destroy its subjects. And it's successful not just because it's powerful, but because its subjects *wish* to be destroyed. We simply desire to be destroyed because it's unbearable to live in the lie.

"That ancient sophism *if I say that I'm telling an untruth, I have told the truth* is no longer valid. It's been removed from circulation. Even the one who secretly scatters ashes on his head and repeats that ancient nonsense is lying. Perhaps he's honest to a point, but he's sorry to miss the comfort of life in the horror of self-deception. It sounds absurd to you, but it's true. Horror is man's basic motive. In order to be able to live, a man must put up with horror or create it. To destroy, either himself or others—it's all the same. And at least that's not difficult; there are hundreds of ways available: drinking (which is practiced here), taking drugs, killing, working, not working, restraining oneself, debauchery, and even train wrecks. Precisely. There is no such thing as accidental destruction. Whenever two trains collide, it's the result of a carefully—Freud would say subconsciously—planned killing, of a horrible conspiracy of the conductor, stationmaster, incidental passersby, and future witnesses to the accident. Because in a world where truth ruled, train wrecks would be simply impossible, just as their existence would be pointless and therefore ridiculous. What's the point of trains in a world where everything is in its place? What else is movement other than fleeing the scene of the crime?"

"Mr. Mercier," shouted Lama Tikhonov, "you're an existentialist!"

Mercier laughed.

"No, I'm a corpse."

"Is there any hope?" the fainthearted bishop asked.

"Fortunately," Mr. Mercier said, "instead of God, Nietzsche died and is now resting in relative peace. Perhaps he finally did understand that God isn't the one who brought death into the world, that people die not because God wants it to be so but because that's what they want; they want to destroy themselves in order to avoid the nightmare of their very own inauthenticity, caused by their undaunted lying. I don't see any other reason why people would die anyway. Nothing else in the universe dies. Except animals. But only at first glance. What else is that mimicry of certain species, all the sneaking around, hiding and hunting, but depravity and lying? We shouldn't be deceived: animals are only a little bit better than people."

I cast a glance at Bishop Van den Garten. With a shaking hand, he was raising a glass of vodka to his mouth. Obviously it was unpleasant for him to listen to the blasphemous theory of a corpse. A—better said—body. It's enough that the dead are dead; there's no point in calling them names as well. But Mercier was not just an ordinary corpse. He was an exceptional corpse, as opposed to the rest who lie listlessly around just as soon as they die. Thanks to the fact that he'd given himself over mercilessly to debauchery, he wasted his soul down to the last penny for a few years before his fate-appointed day, and he was offered the chance to spend a while longer on the face of the earth in the form of an intelligent zombie. And ultimately, why not? He wasn't using any air, he ate nothing, he spent all his money—on vodka at that, which he constantly poured into himself and which simmering there in his stomach like uranium in an atomic reactor, gave him the energy to move about. Because Mercier only comforted himself with hell. If there is no soul—there is no hell or heaven either. When the playoffs are over—destination nothingness. Perhaps that was his goal. Who knows? In any case, he was a refined gentleman from whom one could always hear a multitude of interesting things. To his credit, he was not a hypocrite like Van den Garten. Oh, those Protestants. The bishop figured out how to outwit God. He bought a Sony voice recorder, recorded several prayers, and from time to time he'd turn the apparatus on and humbly listen to the Lord's Prayer. Perhaps I should have let him get lost in his own damned dream and be afraid of hysterical little girls in his nightmares. Or to shoot him, cut off his tail, and take the reward issued by the Holy See. I could just imagine it: the bishop lying in the snow, and I'd have my picture taken with my rifle raised high and self-satisfied grin on my face. But I gave up on the plan. It just wasn't Christian.

God had, anyway, already punished him enough. Like all the rest of us, in the end. And it's obvious that this is just the beginning and the minimum of what we deserve.

"People whose internal time runs faster than the external, they're the ones who drive history," Mr. Mercier was saying. "I also belong to that cursed sort. Of course, I'm completely unimportant. Our kind comes directly from the time of the construction of the Tower of Babel. Like all the others. Because of the enormity of the works, the constructors were forced to divide into guilds. The most zealous champions of the construction, the black magic priests and architects, are the forerunners of today's Sons of Space. The defining characteristic of those people is that they have grandiose plans and an unbreakable will, but due to their limitations (which apply to all sons of Adam), their projects usually end up flopping. In fact, with the development of technology, they gave up on building the tower which was visible; I mean that, turning away from the construction of a building on the face of the earth, they undertook the more perfidious project of converting the entire earth into the Tower of Babel. Operations are constantly ongoing, twenty-four hours a day, in all places. Nobody notices it because of our obsession with everyday events. All the wars, unrest, rebellions, demonstrations—all of that is *organized* so that, via radio and TV, the common people are kept distracted. That, let's call it strategic, turnabout in planning arose in the seventeenth century when they realized that a single building, no matter how large, would not reach the desired height; it was necessary to universalize the project. Yet it would be incorrect to assume that it's even the tiniest of secrets that the people whose internal time runs faster than the external are a closed organization. Most of them aren't even aware that they differ from other creatures in any possible way. They even make use of the other two kinds of people to execute their plans.

Because those for whom internal and external time are synchronized are the offspring of the loyal builders, masons, carpenters, and stonecutters who dutifully participated in building the tower. These people are pragmatists with their feet planted on the ground, adaptable to all changes, never questioning the goal, uninterested in the purpose of what they are doing. By the nature of things, they are the most numerous. Both in that era and today.

But there were always those who didn't forget God's law, for whom official time was restrictive, who did not feel good in the spaces of this world. Those are people whose internal time flows slower than the external. From the offspring of that group, who did in fact participate in the construction but constantly carried out subversions, we now have introverted oddballs, saints, mystics, poets, hobos, and visionaries.

Thus, dear gentlemen, as the Preacher says: nothing new under the sun. The conflict of those three groups have gone on since the very beginnings of history: the first attempt to make the world solid, tangible, unchangeable, the second wholeheartedly aid them in that, the third are constantly subverting everything. All the rest—history, science, social upheaval—is just an everyday circus whose meaning is the same as it was in ancient Rome. The masses should be given bread and, if possible, meat; rebellions and wars are just gladiator games, and that's why they are put on to begin with. Von Clausewitz can write whatever he wants: wars are in no way the extension of politics, they're the simple satisfying of the eternal human need to observe the agony of another human being and enjoy scenes of blood being spilled.

Good Lord, I thought later, lying in bed in my room, that corpse is, judging from all the evidence, actually right. His conclusion was supported by the memory of an event a few so-called years ago, which I intentionally and consciously forgot so that I wouldn't become a schizophrenic. Namely, one evening I drank a lot and before dawn I was trying to return home. "Jesus walked on water," I thought, "and I'm not even able to drag myself to bed. Yep, that's what it means to live in the dark times." That night I drank a lot so I could talk. When tipsy, I fluently speak several languages; when sober, I can hardly speak my mother tongue. That's how ashamed I am to speak. And I'm not quite sure what my mother tongue is: all of them have been ruined. If I remember well, a girl was sitting next to me in a cafe and we were chatting a bit. Was it really just a bit? I left the house as a young man, and I had already become a mature man with a furrowed forehead and crow's-feet. It disturbed me that, when I finally find my place in this world, to the question *where have you been all these years,* I will have to come up with stupid justifications: *I was playing with the kids in front of our building* or *I was part of a work brigade.* In any case, the girl was not attractive; she'd already played several stand-in roles in my earlier books and everyone had given her the thumbs-down, from the director of Prosveta Publishing to the lowliest typesetter at the Radiša Timotić Press; that's the way it is in the world of show business. Perhaps it wasn't even the same girl, but rather falsely introducing herself as someone else; perhaps it was nothing at all—the possibility that I was talking to myself is not out of the question. But we were talking, my memory can't trick me that much, about American football, Frank Sinatra, astrology, chiromancy, Jung, macrobiotics, orgasm, Fidel Castro, Spinoza . . . Now, whatever the case, it would be good to reach my bed. But there was no reference point, no azimuth in sight. The artificial horizon was spinning like crazy. If I had by chance been an airplane, I would've crashed and shattered in a hundred pieces. As it was, I was at least hovering halfway between the bar and my bed, wondering: what am I to do?

First, I lit a cigarette and sat on a low wall beside something irrelevant to the narrative, irrelevant to anything. That was the jubilee two-trillionth Marlboro, lit back in 1978, and I was supposed to get a prize of the newest model Ferrari, but how could I have known that? In the end, I really wasn't even interested. For at that moment I saw only two hundred yards from downtown Bajina Bašta, officially situated in the middle of the Balkan ravines, a seascape, and on the open sea several white sails. I never dreamed that delirium could be so beautiful. The layout of the streets, though still the same, was bordered by different houses where lights were going on, and instead of the hideous post office building, there rose a huge church. Not even a trace of that malignant, metastasized mold, of the disintegrating mortar that laid bare the skeleton pillars of the houses, of the mud being tramped about by chickens. I loitered about those streets, taking in the details, actually checking by way of my impoverished sense of touch that I wasn't dreaming.

If this is delirium—I thought—then I would like never to return to the world of sober, boring, loyal families, the party, the people, and the currents of the revolution.

Of course, it was not a delirium at all. Quite simply, alcohol had so degreased my brain and nerves, had so cleaned them of sedatives and hallucinogens, that for a moment I saw the world as it really is—that is, as it was before the cartographers, librarians, and their minions fixed it into a place of desperation, into a muddy sty, with the purpose of making people irritable, despondent, and evil. Although dead, Mr. Mercier was absolutely correct: they distorted space, moved places around, made a mess of topography in order to create a world just for themselves, a world without God or the law in which, in exchange for eternal life, they could do whatever they liked. Building the tower had gone so far and come so close to the malicious end of construction that they no longer even bothered much to hide themselves. Madmen, drunks, and children are allowed to peer behind the scenes every once in a while, for the simple reason that no one believes them at all. But why would I rack my brain about that if the Government and the responsible ministries don't concern themselves with it?

It began to dawn. I drank down a glass of vodka and turned over, pretending to sleep.

The next morning I was awakened by an official messenger of the Ministry of Information, who delivered an invitation to the public burning of a witch. The company of gentlemen from the previous evening was already sitting at the aperitif bar, drinking down the morning dose of vodka to shake off their hangovers. Somewhat dreamily, with the buzzing in my empty skull, looking at Charlotte Rampling in her armchair, I wondered: is this a novel or delirium? The burning was scheduled for eleven o'clock. The astrologers had made the decision. It was just nine thirty. I had time to drink a few glasses and get my wits about me. Because if things keep going like that, when I return from this shitty country to the shitty country I came from, I'll end up in the insane asylum and no one will believe a single word of what I say. Not to mention there'll be absolutely no writing. Who ever saw a typewriter in the madhouse? There are none for precaution's sake. Indeed, lunatics are placed in asylums so that they won't replicate and spread unpleasant truths. To be honest, they didn't lock me up because journalists aren't as liable to be believed as the insane—even if journalists enjoy some social prestige. But they did come up with a way of disabling me. A sort of house arrest. No one in the whole town wanted to sell me anything or buy anything from me; the really dedicated ones pretended not even to notice me—so I usually sat in my room and carved a mark on the wall for each passing day like a prisoner. I had the right to drink, to travel abroad, to publish my fiction, but for me to walk around town—that was looked at askance. They provided me regularly with electricity, water, food, cigarettes, matches . . . They figured that, sooner or later, I'd wind up dead from cirrhosis of the liver. All of my necessities were brought to me two or three times a week by the municipal clerk, who introduced himself as Nik. AA nickname for Nikola or for nix? The Devil only knows. He looked down his nose at me, with a mixture of contempt and pity, the way insignificant office workers do because there's someone in a worse position than they are, and who sooner or later fall into some sort of dark hole, or get run over by a truck. Or die from a stroke. And that's precisely what happened to Nik one day. Suddenly too. But first, as he was returning to the office after he'd delivered the package to me, he fell in an open manhole. And survived. They pulled him out somehow, he cleaned off the mud and went on, only to be run over by a truck at the very next pedestrian crossing. They took him to the hospital, set his leg, put it in a cast, and just when everything looked OK, Nik had a stroke and died.

"See how meaningless life is and how you should place all your hope in God and not be prideful," said Bishop Van der Garten, who'd started drinking a lot in our company, and kept trembling. If he ever wakes up again in Amsterdam during a fit of abstinence, I wouldn't want to be in his shoes.

"*Sabadhana dukna ti,*" said Lama Tikhonov. He probably meant to say *sabadhanam anićća ti*—that all beings are inconstant, but got confused.

They heard everything. As hungover as I was, I was thinking aloud. What difference did it make? None of the Mongols could understand me, and I intended to tell my friends everything anyway.

"You see," Dr. Andreotti said, "I wouldn't rule out the possibility that you caused that clerk's series of misfortunes. Of course, not by your own will, but subconsciously. You wanted Nik to die, you hated him and, the next thing you know, it actually happened. The power of the subconscious is underestimated."

"I wouldn't agree," was Mr. Mercier's opinion. "The man's time had simply run out. He knew that subconsciously, and that was why he kept trying to get involved in an accident: falling into a manhole, breaking his leg, but no one can get away from destiny."

That morning I was talkative. I was thinking too much.

I found out about Nik's misfortune from the man who was continuing his humanitarian mission in connection with me. His name was Lubarda. Like everyone else with that name, he was a painter. Amateur. He showed me some of his miniatures—some sort of landscapes covered in snow, scattered with little houses whose windows emanated yellowish light. Lubarda wasn't that bad. I guess because he was an artist. But, though it wasn't his fault, the content of the packages was getting poorer all the time: pates, melba toast, ersatz coffee, an egg or two. There must have been an economic crisis raging outside. In any case, they had a formal justification: Officially, I was a social case and—according to the municipality's version—I didn't appear in public out of shame, because I drank a lot, and because I always destroyed every piano I could get my hands on—all of which was essentially true. In the end, it went on like that for about three months and then they forgot about me. And poor Lubarda was executed by firing squad.

"Firing squad!" Van den Garten was taken aback. "Why?"

"For Trotskyism."

"That's terrible. In what kind of vandal country were you living? Unbelievable."

In fact, Lubarda wasn't executed because of Trotskyism. I don't know why he was shot. I actually don't know if he was shot. I lied. I made it up, just as I made up most of my monologue, which is an extremely unpatriotic gesture. But I am not a patriot. After all, it's not as if the number of nameless people is small—those shot for Trotskyism or just by the by, as a way to train inductees. I said that somewhere already: nothing can be made up.

At that moment, Charlotte Rampling passed us. She looked at us with her cold green eyes and asked: "Well, boys. Aren't you going to see the fire show?"

On the main square of Ulaanbaatar, the stake had already been prepared. A rather large pile of wood coated in buffalo oil with a post in the middle. The people were slowly gathering. As foreign correspondents, we got places in the VIP seats where the view of the place of execution was most beautiful. Clerks of the Press Center handed out brochures with facts about the convicted witch and her crimes—a list of buffalo, horses, yaks, goats, and sheep that died because of her curses; the names of people who got sick because of her spells. And finally, the greatest crime: the storm she conjured up out of spite, the very day I arrived in Mongolia, and because of which a reputable meteorologist had been executed. Since the investigation proved that it really was supposed to be a sunny day had evil powers not intervened in the movement of winds and clouds, the meteorologist was posthumously rehabilitated. The rehabilitation ceremony was currently in progress: four members of the National Guard stood next to a picture of the meteorologist, and some sort of official read a long and, apparently, touching speech, because his family members were crying. At the end, the widow was presented the highest medal. Now the execution could begin.

The witch didn't look like a witch at all. She looked like any other Mongolian woman, because they all look alike, just as one egg resembles another. Not losing sleep over it, they could have easily burned any of the women present. At least in terms of visual effect. I simply couldn't get over the impression that they would, in fact, burn any one of them, just randomly. The woman didn't look upset at all. Oriental fatalism. Perhaps. But I would actually guess she was encouraged by the hope that she, too, sooner or later, would be posthumously rehabilitated. At the very least, at the moment when the regime changes. They tied her to the post, and then came the inevitable reading of the sentence, endless and boring, especially if you don't understand a word of it. However, the Mongols weren't bored. They loudly approved certain passages of the high state official's speech. Just around twelve thirty, after numerous rituals, the fire was lit. The oil-coated wood burst into flames and the witch vanished in the flames in the blink of an eye.

After the execution, we dropped by the Star of the East bar, in one of the more elite quarters of Ulaanbaatar, which was visited mostly by Russian experts and Mongolian pop stars. Several of the officers present greeted Lama Tikhonov. An officer is an officer.

We ordered a bottle of vodka. That evening, Scheherazade was Lama Tikhonov.

"Why is there so much conflict in the world?" Tikhonov began his speech theatrically, as only a Russian can. "Why the lack of harmony and understanding? Since when can a father sleep with his daughter, or a brother with his sister? All of those evils start with the exile of the dead. Up until the eighteenth century, the cemeteries were in the heart of every town; you can read about it in the works of many historians. As early as the following century, suddenly and inexplicably, necropolises were moved out to the periphery and became despised places. We began to fear our dead. They became unpleasant for us, we got rid of them and placed them in luxurious depots. That's how far we fell. Because, remember. A man who can't bear death can't bear anything. Everything bothers him.

"Death is completely neglected. Shoved into the background. Nobody thinks about it until they're dying. And by then it's too late. This should be carefully considered: if we have excommunicated the dead, does that mean we've gotten them off our backs forever? Certainly not. We the living carry death in us just as much as the dead carry life. They don't give up quite so easily. I discovered that one evening during *samadhi*. The dead have organized themselves, formed trade unions and committees, and we shouldn't forget that they have numerical superiority. They are rebelling, and most rightly so. What kind of awful segregation is this? Why should someone be excommunicated from society just because they've died? Is illness the ultimate limit of human tolerance?

"Such an undiplomatic attitude toward the dead is a two-edged sword. A dead man and a living one are complementary, like male and female. And therefore, I'm warning you, we should expect a rebellion by the dead, dissatisfied with their status. I shall repeat: they're incomparably more complex than us, the living, and soon this world will be caught up in a series of cataclysms which will, in vain of course, serve as a forewarning. Here is an example: in Ukraine there's a small town, Chernobyl, where I served as a warrantee officer. But in Chernobyl there's a nuclear power plant which provides electricity to Soviet factories and citizens—and also legitimacy and self-assurance to its managers so that they can continue down the path to certain destruction. Before much time had passed, there was a breakdown at the power plant. Just remember how many dead atomic physicists there are, how much knowledge they have, but they are invisible, then relate that to the Book of Revelations 8:10–11: "And the third angel sounded, and there fell a great star from heaven, burning as it were a lamp, and it fell upon the third part of the rivers, and upon the fountains of waters; And the name of the star is called Wormwood: and the third part of the waters became wormwood; and many men died of the waters, because they were made bitter." In Ukrainian, "Chernobyl" means wormwood, a bitter herb. The dead will destroy this world which despised them and expelled them to the regions of darkness, in Freudian terms called *the unconscious* or *the subconscious . . .* "

Who knows how long Tikhonov would have lamented the fate of the dead, if something quite distressing had not happened. At the very mention of the word *subconscious*, Mr. Mercier disintegrated, dispersing from the barstool like a bag of sand. All that was left of him was a pile of earth soaked in vodka. And an envelope addressed to me with the note: *open in three years.*

We drank the rest of the vodka and headed for the hotel.

Before we parted to go to our rooms, Dr. Andreotti told me to visit him at ten in the morning.

A Psychoanalytical Session in a Room at the Genghis Kahn Hotel

Dr. Andreotti's room had been rearranged into a psychoanalyst's office with all its frightening props, including a human skeleton and volumes of books with golden imprints whose pages were—as is generally known—blank. As in all my books, a picture of Sigmund Freud hung on the wall.

Dr. Andreotti got right to the point.

"Do you want to undergo psychoanalysis?"

"Yes," I said, although I didn't want to, but I always answer like that. I never want to, but I always say "yes."

I lay down on the couch. Dr. Andreotti turned on the tape recorder.

Dr. Andreotti: Try to describe for me your earliest childhood memories.

I: A warm summer night. I'm lying in bed and at one moment, in the star-dappled heavens I see six bright disks flying from the west to the east at breathtaking speed. Nowadays that's called a UFO.

Dr. Andreotti: Yes. Nowadays that's called a UFO. Why do you think . . . Maybe it's better to try it like this: why do you wish to be in Mongolia?

I: Because it's far away.

Dr. Andreotti: An honest answer. The wish to flee from one's self. To a greater or lesser extent, everyone has that wish. That's not sick at all. But is that all?

I: What do you mean, is that all?

Dr. Andreotti: I mean—is that your only motive?

(A pause.)

I: No, it's not . . . In fact, I've written this whole story about Mongolia in order to throw the security services off the trail. I thought: when they search the drawer of my desk and find the manuscript . . . When they read it, they'll think: Basara has gone back to his old topics, his obsessions. He's thrown in the towel on the Evangelical Bicyclists of the Rose Cross. As the plot of the novel developed further, they stopped spying on me, and in the second part I could finally finish the trilogy on the falsifiers' conspiracy.

Dr. Andreotti: Conspiracy!?

I: It's generally known that I'm obsessed with conspiracy theories.

Dr. Andreotti: Conspiracies do exist, after all.

I: Sure. My two previous books were falsified at the printing house . . . Perhaps the proofreaders also meddled with the text. Who knows?

Dr. Andreotti: It's more likely that you're the falsifier.

I: I?

Dr. Andreotti: Forget it. We'll talk about that later. Now tell me in detail what your intentions were. How would the novel move forward?

I: I wanted the second part of the book to contain a scholarly work, not an artistic one, but to still be fiction. I have an idée fixe that fiction must become scholarship, a science. But even more than that: it should be a formula, a matrix, according to which the lousy remains of reality can play themselves out. That means authentic history, not the clumsy foretelling of the past from the pens of corrupt historians.

Dr. Andreotti: But on several occasions you've declared your belief in God.

I: That's true.

Dr. Andreotti: That's contradictory. You're assigning yourself a right that only belongs to God.

I: I never considered it. And still, writer-mimics have caused great damage to history. Much more so than historians.

Dr. Andreotti: Explain!

I: You see! Rational speculations about the past causes damage to the present itself. But imagination, that powerful force about which naturalists remain purposefully silent, once projected onto the past, penetrates much more profoundly into the metaphysical tissue of history and influences the future precisely by causing dilettante historians to make the wrong judgments, and based on those judgments the sons of space draw even more incorrect conclusions, thus acting in a way that sailors would if they oriented themselves according to broken compasses. Thus every generation makes ever more catastrophic mistakes.

Dr. Andreotti: Now let's change the subject. Do you keep a diary?

I: I tried to. Don't know how many times. I never managed to keep one for more than a day or two.

Dr. Andreotti: Is that because you don't believe that days exist anymore, or because you think it's enough that an event happens once and disappears into the past?

I: Fifty–fifty.

Dr. Andreotti: But you still go on writing something here and there.

I: Always. It's indeed in vain, but then again so is everything else. Perhaps even more so. Because there's always the hope that someday I'll stumble, by chance, across the thread that snapped in my soul and thus made it impossible for me to bare my soul even on paper. Perhaps rightly so. Paper is a fairly unreliable confessor. If nothing else—if not that—then maybe to relieve the tension which, I must admit, really bothers me, and makes me do careless things from time to time . . .

Dr. Andreotti interrupts me: Like what?

I: For example, I get tipsy, bump into a priest, and ask him if he believes in God; or once in a while, in secret, I approve of some action by the party in power; or I swear like a sailor; or, for example, purely on a whim I don't keep an appointment . . .

Dr. Andreotti: I'm not impressed.

I: Me either. Later, I feel guilty.

Dr. Andreotti: Why?

I: Because I'm a bad Christian. I'm too lazy and weak to resist any sort of temptation. Too lazy to bear my own cross, too much of a coward (I'm afraid of hell) to openly switch over to the camp of sinners and enjoy myself like a man, although I secretly collaborate with them under the mask of drunkenness, as if God couldn't see through that. If even this-worldly judges do not allow inebriation as a mitigating circumstance, why would God? That's just the way it is. I'm neither as god-fearing as I should be, nor do I happily indulge in my vices. A Hamlet-like dilemma for a worn-out civil servant who has even begun wearing ties.

Dr. Andreotti: Just awful!

I: But, unfortunately, true. I actually have eight ties. One of them is even silk.

Dr. Andreotti: What color?

I: Does it matter?

Dr. Andreotti: Colors have their own symbolism.

I: I think the predominant color is blue.

Dr. Andreotti: Blue is a nice color . . . Are you nostalgic about some of the earlier periods in your life?

I: Sure. I miss the time when I used to eat sweet stuff first, and then smoked sausages. The time when I used to bark at city buses. The time when I used to go on long walks in solitude. It was common for me to walk up to fifteen miles completely alone and not be bored for even a moment.

Dr. Andreotti: Were you just walking? Did you do anything else?

I: Well, I'd stop to rest from time to time. In some deserted place. Far from the eyes of people. I'd smoke a cigarette, find a stone, a smooth one or one that was flat enough, and then I'd write a girl's name on it with a fountain pen, and return the rock to its place. I believed that the little forest gods—I was an animist at the time—would do something; that, in her dreams, they would make her—I have to use a cliché—fall in love with me.

Dr. Andreotti: Who was the girl?

I: I don't know. Her father was a military officer. That was all I knew about her. And that she lived in the building next to mine. The window of my room and the window of her room were twins.

Dr. Andreotti: You want to say they were at the same height?

I: Precisely.

Dr. Andreotti: Why did you mention that her father was an officer? Was that so important?

I: For me at the time—yes.

Dr. Andreotti: Why?

I: I envied him for his self-confidence. To this very day I think it's ontologically most advantageous to be an officer in someone's army, a communist one if possible. That's the place with the least ephemerality. The least change. Perfect order. A sort of this-worldly eternity.

Dr. Andreotti: You could have enrolled in the military academy.

I: Impossible. I was a bad student. And anyway, I can't stand discipline.

Dr. Andreotti: And what attracted you to the girl?

I: Exhibitionism. She kept walking around her room naked, and she knew that I was watching.

Dr. Andreotti: You had binoculars?

I: No. Then I could zoom in with just my eyes. To this day, I see far above average. Too well, in fact. I see things around me and they are all, mainly, awful, depressing, or ugly. Who knows, when you look at things well, perhaps they can't be any other way?

Dr. Andreotti: How did you know that she knew you were watching?

I: I just told you. I could see her as clearly as I see you. She gave me obvious hints that she was aware I was watching; she winked at me, smiled at me, sometimes stuck out her tongue at me.

Dr. Andreotti: Describe her room to me.

I: So many years have passed, but I'll try. It was quite a normal room in one of those terrible buildings from the end of the sixties. I think that the building still hasn't been torn down, though I wish it had been. On the floor, if memory serves, there was some sort of carpet or rug. More likely a carpet. From my vantage point, to the left was her bed. No. A couch. On the other side, there was a large mirror. Next to it was a bookshelf, and on the shelf there was one of those awful dolls from Trieste . . .

Dr. Andreotti: Why awful? What can be awful about a doll?

I: Those dolls were far too lifelike.

Dr. Andreotti: Go on.

I: There were two pictures hung on the wall: a portrait of Josip Broz in his marshal's uniform; next to him was a blowup of a bearded man holding a cigar. At the time I thought it was her grandfather, but then a few years later I figured out it was a picture of Sigmund Freud. I have forgotten the details. I paid no attention to the furniture. As I said: I was obsessed with her appearance, more precisely—her nudity. But that's not all. She often had the habit of, naked as she was, sitting on the edge of the couch, raising her legs, bending them and spreading them, and then, in the mirror, studying the morphology of her pussy that she'd spread open with the long translucent fingers of both hands . . .

Dr. Andreotti: Did you love her?

I: Who?

Dr. Andreotti: That girl.

I: No!

Dr. Andreotti: I don't understand. Why do you keep talking about her? A man isn't crazy just because he watches a naked woman.

I: That's beside the point. In those days I knew nothing of the vaginal labyrinth, and I truly longed to learn about it. Do you see: no matter how I stood, I couldn't see the reflection in the mirror from my window. Yeah, and somewhere I came across an anatomy book from Russia, and I compared the movement of her fingers with the drawing in the book.

Dr. Andreotti: Again, I don't understand.

I: At least that much is simple. Just like they make airplanes, that's the way Russians draw pussies.

Dr. Andreotti: Now I really don't understand.

I: Have you ever seen a Russian airplane? You haven't. I have, because I did my military service at the airport. Maybe a MiG-21 can fly at Mach 2, and maybe it's the pride of our air force with its wings of steel, but when you look at it up close, THAT thing looks horrible. Large grommets irregularly scattered around on, likewise irregularly shaped, pieces of dirty gray aluminum. What can the drawing of a vagina in an anatomy textbook possibly look like, if one deals with high technology in such a way? I was traumatized by that drawing. I couldn't get my sex life together for years afterward. That pussy, in the book, was truly horrifying.

Dr. Andreotti: Didn't it cross your mind that it was just Soviet propaganda aimed at making sex revolting and thus reducing the birthrate in capitalistic and revisionist countries? Those books, as far as I remember, were beautifully bound, and they were ridiculously cheap. They practically gave them away. The Russians even faked the maps of their own cities.

I: Well, at the time I was too young and indoctrinated. It never even crossed my mind.

Dr. Andreotti: Did things work out later?

I: What things are you talking about?

Dr. Andreotti: Concretely—about sex.

I: Yes. One grows dull with time. Just remember Fuentes's epigraph from the beginning of the travel guide. But then I became religious; the vaginal landscape no longer seemed so repulsive to me, it was just that sex was still odious because now it appeared in the form of a mortal sin instead of a MiG-21.

Dr. Andreotti: You did succumb to it occasionally, right?

I: To be totally honest, yes. Anyway, most things—books, phenomena, food, drink, etc.—are detestable, but I still eat, drink, read, and so on . . .

Dr. Andreotti: That's an interesting topic. I'd like to hear more about your sex life.

I: Impossible. Because of the paradox.

Dr. Andreotti: What kind? I hope it's not aviation-related again?

I: It's not. The paradox is completely prosaic. Namely, I'm able to go to bed with a woman I hardly know, without knowing if she has an STD or not, but there's no way in hell I can talk about that, not even with a psychiatrist. The shame overwhelms me.

Dr. Andreotti: Shame! Now I've had enough of your psychoanalytic nonsense. There's no reason for you to go on lecturing about your traumas deep and wide if you signed a contract based on a percentage of sales and not the length of the book. Look at me!

I started up out of the lethargy I'd sunk into.

Dr. Andreotti was Joseph Kowalsky.

"Hear me out," he said angrily. "You've never been to Mongolia. Quite simply you fell asleep last night, but this isn't even your dream. You've gotten lost in Bishop Van den Garten's nightmare. And being who you are, you immediately accepted as your own all the hallucinations of a frustrated Protestant clergyman. It's time for you to wake up. You have to go back to all those things and people you've neglected and forgotten. You have to remember everything. Just hang all this babble about salvation through literature out to dry. God has a bad opinion of your books. Of books in general. You have to become a realist. You have to start writing like Tolstoy . . .

Completely drenched in sweat, I woke up, sat on the edge of the bed, covering my face with my hands; that's my usual pose for *samadhi*.

I looked out the window.

It was raining cats and dogs.

I'm pacing up and down the room. In fact, I'm walking back and forth, just so I won't mistake myself for a gnat. I made sure it wasn't raining by closing the curtains and taping them to the windowsill. The drumming of the raindrops doesn't bother me much. All the conditions for a sleepless night have been met. Just waiting for nightfall.

I open the drawer of my desk. The letter I got from my friend is there. Is it possible that I would go so far as to falsify documents, just so I would have a justification for my fantasies and dreams? No matter what Kowalsky says, I have been away for a long time. The dust was thick everywhere! And I dare anyone to say that I turned the vacuum cleaner bag inside-out and scattered dust on everything! Such stories are a thing of the past; the Cold War is over. Even if it were true that it was all just a dream, at least it was my dream. In any case, it's clear that the Prince of Darkness was meddling in the whole affair: Kowalsky did introduce himself as Kowalsky, but he didn't really look like the original, nor did he emanate the same quietude. No, the dream was mine, and that Kowalsky was my private Kowalsky. Saint Augustine says that a man is not responsible for his dreams. That's good, Chuck, Lama Tikhonov, Mr. Mercier, Bishop Van den Garten—all of that was material meant for nothing. Therefore, *ad acta*.

The rain stopped. But I didn't open the curtains. An old trick. It hides itself, you open the curtains, and then it starts raining like crazy. But all these years haven't gone by for no reason; I've learned a few things about meteorology. So, I'm pacing up and down the room. The room is mine, the curtains are closed, and I can walk up the walls if I want to, and no innocent passer-by will be shocked. Well, and even if the curtains were open, I have a right to walk wherever I want until someone proves otherwise. Not even the Criminal Statutes of the PR of Mongolia forbid walking along the vertical axis—not in a single article. I'm pacing, therefore, up and down the room. I'm smoking. I'm flicking the ashes all around me (maybe that's the secret to the dust on everything). I keep looking at the clock.

The secret life of Svetislav Basara? Nervousness when faced with the so-called creative act? *Horror vacui*? Backwater boredom?

Lord knows.

At a certain moment, I look at myself in the mirror: a well-known face. Scar on the upper lip. What to do, Basara, infamous hater of time, space, and the unity of action; well-known narrator of things, phenomena, and concepts about which he knows nothing. And all the while, like an ant, busily gathering materials. And here it is—a starting point. The mirror. It's showing me now just as it wishes. It wasn't always like that, but more about that later. This is also material for me, like Michaux's properties. But there isn't anything better. I'll have to listen to Kowalsky. Even when they're in triplicate, the orders of your superiors are still valid. In keeping with that, I should go back into the past. But I'm even more afraid of the past than of the future. Yes, I can walk up and down the walls, not breathing for days—but the past? It makes me panic.

Why?

Skillfully avoiding an answer, I turn on the desk and sit down. I sharpen a pencil, open a notebook, tear out a sheet of paper. I light a cigarette. I pretend to write something. I always do the same thing. Didn't John Climacus say, if I'm not mistaken: pray, pray without ceasing, the results will come later. A tried and trusted system. Muss up your hair, act like a writer, simulate neurosis, act like you're writing, and all at once the sentences begin to flow from me—nonsense—the Holy Spirit begins to dictate, and thus a novel is born. Yet is there anything at all in my past? There is. There must be. Not because I want it to be so, but because the order of the time-space world is such: there are no gaps in the continuity. If I'm here now, I must have been somewhere else earlier. What a bunch of scholastic sophisms. Grossman would envy me.

And if such a person really existed, he'd even be proud of me.

I have no other choice. Once again, I must seek asylum in the childhood I so recklessly abandoned, one might say without travel documents, enticed by the curriculum and program, by television and American films filled with gorgeous women on the bright sandy beaches of Florida. For starters, whom will I meet there? And, will they see me as a stranger, or just as a lost sheep who's strayed? Ask Knežević? But how? Instead of his telephone number, he accidentally left me his license plate number, and no one knows anything about it. Ask. I'll ask Kukić? Too late. He's asleep. Not ask anyone? Okay, let's see what I've got. A mirror, my childhood, a couple of people . . . Little, indeed very little . . . How can I make a novel out of such crap? But I have written whole novels out of even less. Actually, this gathering of materials is what's confused me so. Do I really want to prove anything to anyone? Far from it. I never have. It's just that I've started liking to document things in recent times. What can be done? The years, the Iron Age, the Year of the Iron Dragon, historicism, solidification, deindividuation, and the other shit from the catalogues of Derrida, Culler, it's all in conspiracy against me. Actually, things are going fairly well. I'll see those dudes who are still writing at the very End of Literature.

And now there's a war on as well. In my dreams I hop over to Ulaanbaatar and they go to war. Miraculously, the mayor of Belgrade and his entourage aren't demonstrating like his predecessors used to whenever a Rwandan lieutenant or the like fired off a clip in the air. To the contrary. But the war doesn't start. The topic is worn out. I'll follow Kowalsky's instructions. With the stroke of a pen, I could put a stop to the bloodshed, but what's the point? Sooner or later, they'll dig up their battle-axes and settle accounts.

What, moreover, am I to do with that person of female gender who's been systematically hounding me for decades by never appearing, even though she ought to? There's nothing more for her to fear. So many years have passed, I've made peace with the idea that I'll remain a bachelor, so I won't mistreat her . . . It would be nice if we could meet at least. Perhaps, aware of the change in circumstances, she'd actually show up this time, but she's ashamed of her crow's-feet and who knows what else. Just like I can't close one eye at a time. If the situation demands—I can close both of them.

How else could I deal with all the stuff rotting on the steppe around Ulaanbaatar? In any case, an interesting topic. Workable material.

All right. I don't doubt that I'll research the causes of the lack of synchronicity, for which I will not accuse her a priori. I'll document it all, black on white. Still, patience is needed. That's why I'm pacing up and down the walls, in spite of this world's logic, chain-smoking. Strictly speaking, there's nothing illogical in my movements for the adherents to the Ptolemaic view of the world. The earth as a flat plate. Many things are different in the laws of physics in that case. But a world set up like that wasn't suitable for adventurers, for the evil-doers who were dissatisfied that everything was in its place, for those who wanted to sail around the world. The globe,—that's the final state of the Dark Ages. What sort of stability can be expected over an enormously enlarged billiard ball? Perhaps Mercator (the cartographer, not the retailers) did a lot for trade and technology, but not so for spirituality. One can rise only from a flat surface, certainly not from an object whose center can't be defined.

I descend from the ceiling to my desk, sharpen my pencil again, and finally begin to write.

Having passed through my stages as a specter and a mannequin, the place where I was born, Bajina Bašta, was more of a journalistic canard or a rumor than a real settlement. The authorities stuck it on maps, in the farthest corner of Serbia, just to fix the average in the statistical reports. At the time of my birth it was just enormous poppycock, a quagmire on the right bank of the River Drina, the place where the dream of Greater Serbia was fossilized on its victorious march toward the West. From that quagmire, here and there, dilapidated little hovels stuck out, made of a mixture of one part clay, one part straw, and one part crap. The two-story houses of pre-war and, as a rule, dead enemies of the people (my grandfather's house among them) were not popular, and everyone silently ignored them, as if they didn't exist. The words *enemy of the people* echoed ominously in the enormous dark halls overfilled with mourning women in black scarves, tubercular peasants, relatives, Gypsies, waiters, outsiders, members of "the surviving world" as the Party secretary called it, and if we'd lived in a country that recognized God and extra-sensory phenomena, those timid, unnoticeable people, certainly have had the status of being specters.

Those were hard times.

During the war, the Germans deported all the Jews to camps, and there was no one to keep the stores open. In any case, privately owned stores were forbidden. There was nothing to buy. Everything needed, every little thing, one had to invent everything, and dream, to create it out of nothing. Fortunately, hope and imagination had not fallen to the low levels of the present day, and somehow people made ends meet. Not even realizing it, under the guise of a materialistic doctrine, in fact we brought to life the ideas of a certain idle Argentinean. If I mention a Hrönir Christmas piglet, the reference I'm making will be clear. As I was saying, there was nothing, but still everything was under close observation. And when you're born in such a backwater place and time, then it's quite logical that you feel nausea and doubt in your own existence. A nihilist heaven. At first glance. But that was the will of fortune, which decided that I should be a storyteller at a time when there's nothing to be said, nor is there anyone who'd care to listen to what I'm saying. There—that's the root of my animosity toward spatial-temporal signifiers in the narrative model. I, of course, did not want to write, but I had no choice. That is my cross to bear, the punishment for my belief in small forest gods who did small favors and fulfilled even smaller wishes, and in return they lured me ever deeper into the idolatry where I would have ended up like sinful Israel if Kowalsky hadn't shown up one day on the banks of the Drina.

In terms of religious confession, the population was formally Orthodox, but belief in God was never the strong suit of those people. I doubt that even today you could find one of them who even knows what monotheism is. To be fair, on the plateau above the town there was a kind of church assembled from Masonite and cardboard. But it echoed from emptiness. Yet a whole series of obscure cultures flourished, inherited from the Slavs, Illyrians, Gypsies, Wallachians, and the devil knows from who all else. To tell the truth, those woodland gods and *potamoi* (who lived in the river's whirlpools) weren't demanding; they willingly did small favors, healing a scab here or a blister there. But not more than that. Their competence ended there. I'm still full of such superstitions, that primitive magic, and even today—after having been a nihilist, an agnostic, and (now) a believer—I will turn back from a trip if I come across a dead dog. Nor will I ever take a pee in a group of more than three men. For the life of me, I would also never touch a menstruating woman. Superstitions, we shall wave our hands in disgust. However, has anyone ever researched just how many people lost their lives because they didn't turn back after seeing a dead dog? Not to mention the large group of heart patients who don't even begin to think that they are exposed to enormous suffering just because they pissed in a group of more than three. And really, how can one just go to a psychiatrist and say: listen, I'm an alcoholic, and there's nothing I can do about it. Every day I touch several menstruating women in a crowd, but in times like these how can you know who's having their period and who's not? That's exactly how it happens, the touch of a menstruating woman directs us by fate toward the nearest pub. I mean, really, where did all those animistic cults come from? If I strain my memory, after all these years, even today I can remember Celtic lullabies . . . Or the places where grass grows that can make you invisible . . . Look no further. Kowalsky will never come back again. Not a chance.

Still, the communist travel guides offer quite a different image of my hometown. According to them, it's a thriving place where the tobacco, wood, and processing industries are flourishing. In doing so, they quote the facts, and the facts always say the opposite of what I'm saying, and I'm proud of that. All those monographs are overflowing with documents, photographs, decrees, correspondence, and lists. I don't disagree. But come on, let's look at it, how did that merry little town on the slopes of Mount Tara come about? It's all just a trick, a deception. Bajina Bašta is a run-of-the-mill quagmire, and the photographs and documents are created on the principle by which provincial photo studios work. There's no one who doesn't know about those cutouts painted with airplanes, nymphs, luxurious salons, and whatnot, where there's a place for you to put your face. In the same way, in the agitprops, clerks shove their heads into the opening of certain cutouts, the photos are passed on to activists, and they kindly make them available to the historians. That's how, after all, the history of every country and the entire world has been made. It's all just a concoction of atheists, esthetes, and structuralists. Since they're unable to stand the deformity of the world, a deformity which can't be repaired and which causes unbearable nausea, they spend a large part of the gross national product on the production of factsheets, documents, parchments, decrees, and all the other malarkey. They simply can't stand the nausea, which is reasonable: nausea is a sign of religiosity.

There you have it. From a religious standpoint, history differs remarkably from the official history of the state. It's a universal paradigm. Just as, somewhere in the Balkan mud, Nicholas of Cusa came up with the idea of *coincidentia oppositorum*, so it happened to me in the mire beside the Drina, one moonless night as I stared up at the blank sky, that I was overcome with the revelation that all those solid buildings, highways, electric plants, stadiums, circuses, and factories are nothing more than a setup, a peepshow, a panorama created by the atheists, structuralists, and librarians—all of those who can't stand mud. For the simple reason that it's quite obvious that we're in a blood relationship with clay. That clay is, let's say, our brother. In their efforts, the dimwittedness characteristic of the Kali Yuga era fits right into their plans. I've been repeating it for years: look how beautiful the avenues are, and how luxurious the bright lights of the boulevards, how tall the buildings are . . . And the gullible begin to envision what's suggested to them, following the rule that a lie told a hundred times becomes the truth.

Let's take an example. Johan Huizinga writes the book *The Autumn of the Middle Ages*, yaks about all kinds of stuff on the life, customs, habits, and actions of people in that period. And so what? Supposedly, he reconstructs the past. Far from it. In a way, he forces *Those* people in the eleventh and twelfth centuries to behave in the way the author and his minions think appropriate. Because—and this is very important—it's not impossible to change the past; only the past can be changed. It is impossible to change the future. Directives for the present must arrive from the future because, if it weren't so, the flow of history would never take on such a diabolic direction. And the outcome of that flow is— the transformation of the world into nothing.

Of course, no one notices this. Precisely because we're an integral part of the world, because we're also being destroyed with it, and because it's impossible to observe changes from within a given system. When I mentioned the provincial photo studio, I was thinking of the most primitive principle, not indicating the advancement of technology. Holographs have long since replaced garishly painted sham backgrounds. The world is a hologram. No matter how much of it is destroyed, the remains always contain an image of the entire system with all its details. Already seventy percent of the universe has been transfigured into nothingness through alchemical and structuralist activities, and yet everything is still here: dimensions, the seas, oceans, mountains, stars, and galaxies. With the proviso that all processes are accelerated and that the disorder is ever greater because of the ever-greater distance from the axis and the ever-closer approach to the outer extremities of *chakravarti*. From this, it can be concluded that people are also thirty-percent people, or better said— thirty-percent something. And that *something* can be reduced to the gastrointestinal and genitourinary systems, and the lower brain functions which are reduced to the coordination of physiological processes. Just enough so that we don't shit in our homes and on our streets or have intercourse in public places. So much for ethics. The relics of creativity and imagination have actually been reduced to the convoluted discovery of ways to supply ourselves with as many means of satisfying our physiological wants as possible. Certain authors, whose opinions I certainly hold to, go even further in humiliating modern man (if IT can be more humiliated) and refer back to the ancient myths, according to which the human being was already reduced to fifty percent when the androgen was cut in half—a mythological time even in Plato's day—so that the real price of the average man on the ontological market falls to a total of fifteen percent.

It's a real wonder that such a vague creature can do so many evil and immoral things. This can be explained—in a comforting way, at that—just by saying that evil has no reality in itself, that it is *nothing*, so that as the world and its wretched inhabitants are annihilated more and more, evil flourishes, like cancer cells, only to destroy itself in the end. That which is, is forever. And it is not here. Nor there. Out of pure mercy it appears in this nothingness just so that everything doesn't plunge into the darkest blackness. At a glance—everything is going on as usual, but the boundary between reality and the media has vanished. We watch the faces on our TV screens, we observe the commentators, announcers, heroes of series and films, but only recently (and only in esoteric circles) has it become known that they are also observing us, following our every step, which the officials of the appropriate *service* carefully record on video tape. Thus, people long dead, recorded on film, have been brought back to life through the corresponding magical techniques and—even though there were honorable people among them—placed in the roles of denouncers. What does a man have to do just to live, in some fashion?

But it's better if I leave my para-philosophical babblings behind, those babblings so characteristic of heavy books. Heavy books are a thing of the past. Who will be the first person I meet on my pilgrimage into the past?

Perhaps the person whom, for lack of personal information, is stored in the archive of my memory under the name of Girl in the Window across the Yard.

In Bajina Bašta, on a shady street that will bear my name many years later (although that brings me no kind of satisfaction), there was a yellow, dilapidated house, and it had a window. Now, in that window lived a girl, the daughter of the house's owner. Not in the sense that she often stood in the window, as small-town girls often do, she lived there: she did her homework there, played with her ragdolls there, I guess because of the lack of living space. Or because she was being punished. I don't know. I'd see her in the summer because, at the time, I lived in another equally remote place and spent summer vacations at my grandma's house. I had the perverted habit—one of many—of wandering around the empty streets during the hottest part of the day. Passing by that mysterious window, supposedly just as a bumbling tourist, I stopped for a few minutes dressed in a redingote, corduroy pants, and a top hat, with my grandfather's ceremonial cane in my hand. Strange clothing for a ten-year-old! But it's worth noting that I've been inclined to eccentricity ever since I was little. This has brought me a lot of trouble in life. Already at the age of seven, I was brought to trial for disturbing the peace.

But before setting off on my walk, I would go to the woods behind my house and make sacrifices to the small forest gods and their Optimus Maximus, who was named Stormy. A few hazelnuts, some orange peels, two or three caramel candies—those tiny offerings were enough for the insignificant daemons to fulfill my wish: that the Girl in the Window across the Yard look at me at least for a moment. In those days, her look was the only thing I could stand. Maybe because she was, in fact, a doll. I reject that presupposition as being baseless. At least one thing had to be something other than a backdrop; at least someone had to be something other than a doll made of papier-mâché. Did I love her? No. And yet I cared about her. That's just the way it is: those you don't know, or see only once in life, you retain in your memory, but those close to you, you more or less hate in secret. Anyway, that street always roiled with interesting things. Visiting circuses put up their tents on its vacant lots, there was a market for salesmen of luting, meetings were held there for the Association of Snake Charmers, that was where the sellers of cornstalk windmills met, and the producers of elderflower flutes—the members of all those guilds which disappeared one after another under the flood of fans of electric energy, iron, and aluminum.

Now, it could be that my affection toward the Girl in the Window of the Yard was quite prosaic in nature, in the literal sense of the word. I wanted nothing from her. I did not intend to ever meet her. In the end, I would have nothing to say to her. All things taken into consideration, I was gathering materials even way back then. It never crossed my mind that I would ever be a writer, but I was already gathering materials. The urge was not so low. Everything I noticed, after many years and rigorous cleanups: found its place in these texts, the goal of which is to save what can be salvaged from the overall process of annihilation. Because, just as God used to speak to people through books, nowadays (since the legitimate ways have been sabotaged) people can address God only through books. And in no other way. And now, when I think of the whole series of my futile feelings of love toward fictional or hardly existing girls, I recognize in it the hand of Providence, which thereby taught me that the only true loves are those which are impossible and unachievable—precisely those which the invisible, hidden, and incomprehensible God appreciates most.

Somehow, at that time, the communists started the great spring genocide. Since they'd long ago wiped out all the human beings who might oppose them, leaving only cowards or awkward fellows (like me), they went to work on the rest. First, the small forest gods perished. Every evening, huge fires were built on the meadows, over which activist bums would jump, all accompanied by the hellish firing of rifles and pistols, from which those fragile creatures expired. Then they killed the stray dogs. So they wouldn't set a bad example. And they're not easily organized. Then they threw out the disreputable clerks, just on an evil whim, one hard to stop once it gets set in motion. Among them was the father of the Girl from the Window in the Yard, who was such an insignificant clerk in such an unimportant office that no one had ever even seen him. Then they went after the forests. After a few months of respite, mementos got their turn. They organized supposed campaigns for cleaning up the town, and they made a big bonfire of countless letters, postcards, herbariums, scrapbooks, and photographs. And there you have it: the secret reason why we have so few mementos.

But still, in the period between two of these round-ups, I managed to save something from the bonfires of those countless St. Bartholomew's Day massacres. One August afternoon, while the peaceful citizens and activists digested enormous quantities of cruelly slaughtered, then baked, chickens, turkeys, and piglets, I committed my first felony: I went into the abandoned house of the Girl from the Window in the Yard. Carefully, so as not to injure the fragile psyches of her ragdolls lying about in the corners, I entered her place of residence. To be fair, it was a broad window, they don't make them like that anymore. Everything was in its place: the bed, the tiny closet in the corner, the miniature desk where I found her journal, a yellow graph-paper notebook, the only document that proved not only that she existed, but that she was also a poet.

Only now, after all this time, I'm reading through the verses, retyping them, and offering them to the wider reading audience:

I know, God is only clinically dead,
he'll recover and go back to work.
In the meantime, we'll pray
to chemistry, physics, and the knowledge
of nature and society.

There are no flowerpots on my windowsill.
At night, I touch my pussy, and in the morning
I mourn for the partridges. (1)
The cracking of whips upon the backs of worn-out
hags, says that the war is still not
over.

Carefully, so as not to injure the fragile psyches
of my dolls lying
in the corners (2), I pace from side
to side in the window. They all see me, both those
inside and

those without. I only see
the black silk of sadness.

I wonder, has God lost
faith in me (3), have my stupidities
gotten on his nerves. And again, I know that
the angels don't love sad people. One should
sin, and not regret, and still be happy.
Let the Devil get drunk in the stinking
village tavern (4).

*

Tonight, they were killing the dogs again
because they didn't go to their military training.
O, the cries and whines of those dogs'
sons made me go on all fours
and weep.

The only thing that would plug my ears
is a big white cock.

I live in a place that doesn't exist.
It was dreamed up from nothing. They passed a
decree.
Everyone else believes that this
town exists, and they could say I'm crazy.
And that's true. But carefully composed
propaganda could convince even

smarter people of even greater nonsense
than our miserable town.

I would feel better if I weren't alive
in a place that does exist. For which
history could be a witness at the court of honor.
Where cathedrals and the shields
of great families represent the place.

And I would feel best nowhere.
Or in Mongolia. In the tent
of some sort of bloodthirsty hunter for
decorations of bone in my hair.

Last night, I dreamt I was climbing
a spiral staircase up to
somewhere. It was a good dream. But the stairs
didn't reach high enough.
In the end, exhausted, I came back
down. Among the dog killers
and the decimators of immortal beings.

The rest of the notebook had been destroyed by the
damp. Many of the pages had been torn out. Still, the
fragment of the poem sheds light on many dark spots in
relation to the Girl from the Window and the Literary
History of Bajina Bašta, which will never be written. It
seems that, despite her miniature dimensions, the Girl
in the Window across the Yard, was quite a bit older

than me. This is testified to by verse (1) *At night, I touch my pussy*. She must have had a strong reason to do so. And strong reasons of that nature usually arise from puberty. Reasonably so, that verse destroyed my last illusions about the female gender. I thought that she was Melusine, but she was, like all the other chicks, just an ordinary cunt with a little bit of poetic talent. It's certain: women don't have a soul. But do I have one? Have I not used some of her ideas in my fiction, like that one about the "fragile psyche of her dolls" (2), or that thing about doubting in God's favor (3)? However, the continuation of that verse is far more interesting, where she lays out her understanding of sin and clarity (4), where she paraphrases the "fool for Christ" monk, Varsonoufie from Solovyov's work, *Three Conversations*. Is it possible that someone was reading Solovyov in 1963 in Bajina Bašta? That this creature, of 15 x 4 cm dimensions, was ruminating on the heavens, sin, and large sexual organs? Oh, where is this Kali Yuga leading us? To be fair, a lot of this can also be attributed to my perversities, but I am the lord of this novel, and I have the right to veto.

Well, what's done is done. I will never uncover the mystery of that girl. I will never come to know what attracted me with such power to that shady street, which will one day be named after me. And I couldn't really give a fuck!

It's nighttime. At least I suppose it's night, because the curtains are drawn for the sake of precaution. Tormented by writing, I'm no longer able to walk across the ceiling. No harm in that. Who would be impressed by that in written form. I could demonstrate this ability in front of an audience as well, but I'm inhibited by horrible stage fright. And ultimately, it's not really a miracle. Walking across the floor—across a horizontal surface in general—is just a matter of habit. A simple convention. No one would ever vote for me if word spread that I can walk across the ceiling.

I look over the pages I've written. Triviality after triviality. A bit of homework that I leave gladly behind, longing for the moment when I can pick up a nice comic book before going to bed. The dusk of postmodernism. Clerical work. To be fair, in the service of Providence. No, in this external history, you cannot find or resolve anything. In that sense, the facts laid out in the first part of this novel, declared to be a dream, should be taken more seriously than these, which are classified under the jurisdiction of reality. And yet the writing must be done. Literary fame doesn't interest me. The opinions of critics even less. I write books so that I can search for *something* in them; not to force my way into Serbian literature, which will very soon turn into a paramilitary organization and therefore not interest me at all.

Even now I don't have a very high opinion of it.

Well, all right, what do I expect in the landfill from which I write, here now for more than fifteen-odd or more years, all the while tortuously trying to maintain the bearing of an author? To play the role, I should

have lost at least twenty-five pounds and be doing a
lot of nonsense that I wouldn't have done otherwise. I
should, for example, be drinking heavily, but I simply
can't stand alcohol. What can be done? The role must
be played professionally. In the end, publishers toss me
a crumb from the table. Never mind, let's return to the
question of what I'm searching for in the hundreds
of thousands of words I've scribbled down. Historical
fact—surely not. Even if you asked me, I'd never mention the Trojan War, the Rise of Athens, or the Fall of
Rome. What then?

    To be honest, I'd talk about a woman. There you have
it—one more argument for the psychiatrists in favor
of the thesis that I'm completely crazy. A man writes a
few books, and then looks for the woman of his life in
them. Doctoral dissertation material. But I'm not looking for just any woman, no matter how pretty, rich, or
educated, no one who might belong to this world. My
ambitions are greater. I'm not at all interested in a particular person; no one who respects themselves appears
in this world—not even under a pseudonym. This is
an El Dorado for nobodies, ne'er-do-wells, cheats, the
cheated, and imbeciles. Truth be told, I feel a certain,
not negligible, attraction to attractive women, but I'm
protected from that menace by the very thought that
each of them will, in 2030, be a wrinkled old hag, or
even a decomposing corpse. Oh, how comforting is
religion.

    But then again—I say to the walls as I light a

cigarette—fiction isn't such a harmless thing. Listen up, dear walls, I cannot say these things to others. A little bit of metaphysical babble about literature is never wasted. I consciously belittle the possibilities that books conceal within themselves. And they are unfathomable. Because subversion begins in the domain of metaphysics. As early as 1981, in *Vidici* magazine and *Student* newspaper, the precise plan of the disintegration of Yugoslavia was made public. For the mayor, central committees, and councils of Belgrade, that was unacceptable. Yeah, and then I stepped onto the stage, together with a few of my pals, and we put all our efforts into the deconstruction of form, the negation of time, and the mockery of spaces. The wise guys in the Department of Modern Literature thought that the state dissolves first, and then from the continuing chaos, sensing the loss of all values, artists begin to deconstruct the forms. All backwards: first the novels begin to fall apart, and only then does the state follow suit. But, I should put aside political discussion because . . .

Here comes my friend (the one who killed himself in the first chapter in order to give me the materials to begin with). I see him through the curtain that selectively lets in only the things I want to see. He's not alone. He's got some sort of female creature with him, so the rumor will get around that he's a real man. He's never without a woman. But it's a fake-out. He finds some gal, pays for her dinner, or gives her a buck to go for a walk with him. Otherwise, he's got just as many complexes as I do. In that letter he wrote before his suicide, the authenticity of which I find a bit dubious, didn't he say that we're like Castor and Pollux? He's coming down the street the urban planners designed just to unload a bunch of specters on my shoulders. Not a moment's peace. Neither in my dreams or in reality. There—I put up with so many troubles in Mongolia, and it turns out that it was all just a dream, as Lola Novaković would say. Then you wake up and, pressured by deadlines, you begin to write, and then someone comes by for a visit.

He's not coming empty-handed. I can see a bottle wrapped in paper. He's bringing me alcohol and writing materials. Stuff for my narration. His uninteresting biography. Zachariah, my friend. An inventor. A loafer, like me, he had to find a profession worthy of respect which didn't make him sweat too much. I became a writer, he an inventor. His Patent YU N2346/79 is legendary: a lighted five-pointed star for officers' caps, with a photo cell which, as soon as it gets dark, activates a bulb inside the star, thus keeping the officers safe from careless drivers. To make things more interesting, the General Headquarters took over the patent, and if things hadn't worked out like they did, at night the barracks would look like Manhattan. In any case, Zachariah got paid his fee. He cooperated with the establishment, no doubt, but with whom else could he deal? Not all of his patents were accepted. His indoctrination room, for example.

However, this time the woman accompanying him

was not a paid escort, but a journalist. A real journalist with huge glasses, a tape recorder, a notebook, a journalist pass on her lapel, a typewriter in her hand, travel papers, and all those little things a good journalist needs. She wanted an interview.

"I don't give interviews," I said.

Zachariah opened the bottle. Finnish vodka. He winked at the journalist to indicate: wait till he gets tipsy, he'll talk all night. If it was night.

"All right," I said. "I can give you an interview, but under two conditions. First: that you don't ask me questions like *when did you start writing*, and *what do you think about postmodernism*. My second condition: ten thousand dinars."

The journalist was taken aback. She looked at Zachariah, he gestured with his hand to indicate I was crazy, which wasn't far from the truth. Don't I pace the ceiling? Didn't I hold my breath for months,* didn't I stand in the middle of the room clenching my fists till they go numb, kill all those leftists and humanists who demonstrate every day because of all sorts of nonsense? In the end, I was flattered that the newspapers were interested in me. It means I exist, and not everything's a dream. But newspapers are even more worthless than dreams. They don't prove anything.

"Come on," Zachariah insisted, "don't be so childish. Tell the girl something about yourself, answer a few questions. Why are you so vain?"

"Not a chance. This is about principles. We can sit

here nicely and talk, drink a liter or two of vodka. I don't want any sort of public exposure. Anyway, I'm tolerating you just because of the ever more frequent complaints that there are no women in my books. And because of the possibility that they'll declare that I'm a fag."

Here, Zachariah broke in.

"In his early childhood he was a goalkeeper. They often scored on him because—I can reveal this now because he's hung up his spikes—he couldn't defend against goals shot to his left. He's always been for the right. So, now, every time he got scored on, the drunken fans in the seats would shout: hey, you faggot! That gave him a complex."

"I thought," the journalist said naively, "that fags were ballet dancers."

"All men are fags," I said bitterly.

"And women?"

"Women are fags, too."

Then I recalled that I forgot about the asterisk where I announced a footnote (*) related to breathing. Well, I thought, instead of writing a footnote, I'll tell the journalist why I hold my breath. Let her write her silly interview.

"You see," I said, "in the periods when I'm subli- mating the materials I've gathered for writing, I have the perverse habit of not breathing for several months. However, it's perverse only at first sight, in fact it's based on a scientific method. True, it's not a method from the

West, I wouldn't give a wooden nickel for that stuff. It's an eastern method. The tradition of the East stands on the idea that, when every person is born, they have a precisely predetermined number of inhales and exhales. That's how I save mine up and lengthen my life . . . But not so I'll live to be as old as Methuselah, but rather to reach an average old age, because between two writing sessions, I mercilessly destroy myself with alcohol."

Zachariah interrupted again.

"Why don't you tell her something about your trip to Mongolia?"

"You were in Mongolia?"

How could he have known I was in Mongolia if I wasn't actually there? Not even a dream is a safe place anymore. Its inhabitants would appear to be snitches, ghosts with permanent seats on the board of dreams.

But I can always use my right to veto.

"I've never been in Mongolia. Zachariah's been drinking and he's starting to babble."

"Can you tell me something about your literary strategy," the journalist insisted.

"Quite gladly. What are you interested in?"

"Your next project."

"You see, that's not easy to explain. In broad strokes, the strategic goal of my novel is of several kinds. First: to selectively gather a certain number of things which deserve to be protected from the leprosy of this world. Second: to create a work that will have almost no reference to the reality of the state. And third: by means of literary manipulation, to introduce into this world a certain number of things, concepts, and beings that do belong to its order."

"What are those things, beings, and concepts?"

"I haven't reached that chapter yet."

Tipsy, Zachariah was giving me signals behind the journalist's back. With gestures he was indicating that he'd like to take the journalist off on one of his pointless and anemic love adventures. I had nothing against it, and they left. I saw them moving away through the curtain, in a direction that would take them into another tortuous night and morning filled with disgust. That's the way the world is. If I weren't writing, I'd join them. I never miss the chance to make a mistake. But I'm writing, banging my head against the wall trying to find a way of keeping my promise. How can I introduce into this world a thing, a concept, and a being which don't belong to its shitty order? I'll figure something out.

It's getting late. I get up, lean against the wall, count to a hundred, and slowly fall asleep.

For as long as I've been self-aware, the plotline of all my dreams has unwound in the magical triangle of Bajina Bašta–Užice–Belgrade. None of the luxury of the dreams of the Old Testament prophets. The overall profanation of the world has taken over the space of dreaming as well, so my own dreams were mostly gray, dull, and rainy, like reality. Except that, in them, the physical laws of nature didn't apply, which isn't a particular advantage, because they lose their meaning in one's waking state, thus preparing for a period of ultimate apotheosis in which *the sons of perdition*, manipulating devaluated reality, will create an illusion of fabulous miracles, and thus seduce the masses.

The critical period in the destruction of dreams was between 1935 and 1958, at the time when the Traumeinsatz was active, along with its double, the Sixth Department of the Russian NKVD—the Commands of the Parapsychological Control of Dreams. The invasions of the agents of the abovementioned organizations into the deepest realms of dreams—without the proper preparations—introduced the spirit of materialism into that subtle world. At the same time, through the cracks which appeared through the penetration of discursive thought into the world of symbols, into reality flooded a bunch of fictitious persons, evil spirits, the specters of suicide victims, who insinuated themselves among supposedly real people. (See more on this subject in *Fenomeni*, Užice 1989, and *In Search of the Grail*, Dalkey, Victoria, 2017, both by the same author.)

Like in reality, in my dreams I was also muddle-headed and superficial. I mostly enjoyed cliff-diving, erotic adventures accompanied by conflict, admiring picturesque and vanishing landscapes. But now that I think about it more, that was under the influence of my lucky star, invisible from earth, Proxima Centauri, lost in the depths of the galaxy, far away from the reach of astrological wonders. Because it's not good to take either dreams or reality seriously. Only much later, when Kowalsky found me on the banks of the Drina one afternoon, did the process of initiation start, so—already well advanced in years—I several times went into the deepest regions of dreams, to the place from which one can see the second of the seven existing heavens. But Kowalsky died, which in a way was only right considering he was about 1350 years old, and I no longer dared to venture by myself into the depths of the uncertain. But when that did happen by accident (because here, too, accidents aren't out of the question), what did I do? I messed it up. I found myself in Mongolia, where I was a nightmare for the freaks who were my own nightmare, and we didn't even know it and acted quite normal, like a group of journalists and playboys—though I must admit, rather prone to a good buzz. And once again, Kowalsky helped me, disguised as the specter of one of Freud's disciples.

Now I'm sitting at my desk. It's midnight, because that's what suits me. I'm trying to recall the things I predicted in my dreams, obsessed by boorish siddhis and the meaningless abundance of devilish poppycock.

For example, the smallest common container of all those dreams was a big, slow river, a steep bank, and the appearance of a female person, right beside me, whom for unknown reasons I never wanted (or dared) to look at. I always skipped that opening scene of the dream, fast-forwarded it as quickly as possible, and set off into dubious adventures from which I awoke with the unyielding desire to hang myself or jump out the window. But now the time has come to confront the face I've been avoiding. It must be that my conscience wasn't clear; why else would I look down, like a guilty man? And why wouldn't I, in the end of all things? Didn't I?

In the abovementioned hallway in my grandfather's house, during my childhood, there were several mirrors from which the silver glazing was peeling, and which were slowly growing dim. In those days, nobody cared much about mirrors. The things that caught the attention of the family made up a dreary inventory: lard, bacon, potatoes, beans, a meter or two of cheap cloth . . . Accustomed to pre-war luxury, then abruptly neglected, those Venetian mirrors began exhibiting visible signs of aberration. First they became introverted, withdrawing into the depths of their deceptive souls, and then they grew completely subjective. Many years later, in a book by an imaginary author, I read that, in the Golden Age, all mirrors were like that, but I couldn't know that back then; in the novel *How the Steel Was Tempered*, there was no mention of that. The only creature in the house of the deceased Svetislav Veizović who paid attention to the mirrors was me. At dawn, or at dusk, I would take a chair, climb up, and stare at what used to be a shiny surface, now covered with grime. And every time I looked in them, the mirrors showed a different face, depending on the mood. Theirs. Not mine. I have to admit that those faces differed markedly from my faces as recorded in the faded photographs I was soon to remove from the albums and feed to the dogs. I trust my memory more than photographs, because photographs, and this shouldn't be forgotten, are documents—evidence of facts. I remember one such face, which I liked the most, because it was sexless, neutral, and toward which I felt a certain amount of affinity. Most of the things I'd later write about I saw in mirrors, so in a sense I'm either a plagiarist or a clairvoyant. Of course, I deliberately forgot all of that eventually, skillfully pretending that I was conjuring up those things from the dark recesses of my subconscious. In other words, I was gathering materials from my earliest childhood. I was just an ordinary clerk of the Evangelical Bicyclists of the Rose Cross, and I guess that's why the remains of conscience wouldn't allow me ever to feel like an artist. And I'm finding that out just now.

Once, in a dream, I looked at the face of that girl who in the opening credits of my dreams, stood at the very beginning, seemingly by accident, like in Buñuel's films. That was one of the faces that my subjective mirrors showed me. As I said, I no longer dared to look at it, but now I wonder: why?

So I ask myself that question, sitting at my desk. I imagine that to the right there's a large candle burning, because I hate to get up and turn on the light. Was that female creature my anima, the visualization of the most refined of the three souls which every human being has? Knowing myself, my infinite capacity for self-deception, I pretended that she was an unimportant detail of my dream, so that I could avoid looking her in the eyes and exposing myself to the hellish torments of being scolded for the foolishness I committed against her, in cooperation with the other two souls, of a lower order: the vegetative and the animal. And I wasted my dreams on what total idiocy of what sort? Well, once, for example, I dreamt that I was kissing Mussolini on the mouth. And in doing so I felt no discomfort whatsoever. Proof of latent homosexuality and a proneness to fascism? Perhaps. But women are also somehow people. Isn't that so?

Here I am again, staring out the window. The curtains are down, but anyway I don't intend to see anything. Ultimately, I know the area by heart, I even feel one neighbor or other passing by. I'm staring into the darkness in order not to write, although I'll have to write eventually, but in the meantime I'm justifying my laziness by simulating melancholy, because of an imaginary memory that's suddenly popped up from the past. It's always like that. As soon as the narration heads in the direction that might reveal a dark corner of my soul to me, I immediately change the subject, I begin the next chapter and start lamenting my miserable fate. It's not hard to find a reason. Let's say, for example, why do I, who was the rhythm guitarist in a provincial rock band, why do I have to be the one to cope with unsolvable metaphysical problems? Am I the one who's charged with the task of establishing whether women have souls or not? And since I'm already dealing with metaphysics, it wouldn't hurt to say this as well: that scholarship is hopelessly out of date, and I'm just complicating my life with the mentalities of the thirteenth and fourteenth centuries, at a time when the following question is what should be put forward: is there any life at all on earth? If there is, is it just a derivate of dreams, or the production of a TV station? Do people exist and, if they do, do men have a soul?

Just next to me is a camera. Russian. Zenit is the brand. I could have gotten a better one, but the rationalist and skeptically oriented cameras of Japanese and American production are out of the question. They could not record anything that their makers didn't believe in. Only a cumbersome apparatus made by an open-hearted Slavic soul is able to photograph the subtle creatures in the deepest regions of dreams. But nothing will come of that. I won't use it. I will not sink into dreams, nor will I photograph that girl on the banks of the Drina (where now corpses are floating in broad daylight) for the simple reason that the guy screwed up who was supposed to make it possible for the girl who drops by the Amstel Café (I think her name is Ana) to lend me a snapshot. But what can be done? A novel is always counterfeit and always a construction, no matter how much the author and his theoretician accomplices strain to prove otherwise. If that is a sort of justification, the abovementioned Ana actually does look like the image of my anima. In the end, mimesis always wins the match.

Well, all right! What can I change in all this? I, who never managed to finish college, to get a driver's license, to build a house, to get an American Express card, to conquer Mount Everest? I didn't even manage to get a photograph of the girl, which would offer the illusion to the naive that I smuggled an object from the dream world into reality. Anyway, the reality–dream dichotomy has become completely devalued. Soon, it will lose all importance. That's what the rules of the New World Order demand. Dreams are a thing of the past. The sons of space are seriously considering expanding the territory of their miserable empires to the region of dreaming. And yet no matter how much I construct/deconstruct, no matter how much I imagine things, I do possess a few documents: the letter from my friend (who most likely didn't kill himself); a photograph of an official document confirming that the Cyclists are not fictional; and finally a letter from Bishop Van den Garten.

All of that will be made public and available for possible expert evaluation.

And again I'm pacing across the ceiling. Carlos Fuentes was right. With repetition, the unusual becomes usual, and things that were common and ordinary in earlier times become portents the moment they cease to be repeated. The ability to walk along a vertical axis no longer excites me. I'm bored, and I'm chain-smoking. There's one awkward question that's been bothering me for days now: the fact that I pace the ceiling, is that *siddhi*, or the simple fact that I'm turning into an insect?

Ultimately, I can always rush over to my desk and write: the end of literature! Period.

TRUST ME, I KNOW WHAT I'M DOING.

The Letter from Bishop Van den Garten

AMSTERDAM
OCTOBER 23, 1991

DEAR MR. BASARA,

War is raging in your country now, the situation is uncertain, and I am not sure you will receive this letter. But after all the things that have happened to me in the last three years, I am no longer certain of anything, and yet I feel good (insofar as my conscience allows), even better than earlier, when I made the ridiculous division: certain–uncertain, and my firm faith in God has returned.

After your sudden and unannounced departure, many things changed in Mongolia; I believe that you have kept up with those changes in the newspapers. In place of the communist regime, a democratic one has now come into existence. A multitude of those anachronistic and absurd laws (which irritated you so) have been revoked, and life

has become much more pleasant, but—unfortunately—
far too European. The government, namely, passed a law
on the basis of which the Republic of Mongolia will be
relocated a whole 8,500 kilometers to the southwest. In
order to draw closer to the ways of the modern world and
to fit into all of the general decadence. With the same
goal in mind, a language reform has been imposed so that
now every third word in Mongolian has been replaced
with the corresponding one in English. The new government has legalized whorehouses and private entre-
preneurship. Of course, religion is no longer seen as the
opium of the people, so I could develop a wide range of
missionary activities, and freely preach the Gospel.

Unfortunately, instead of being interested in religion,
most Mongolians are fascinated by digital watches, televi-
sions, and video recorders. In spite of that, I managed to
organize a fairly strong Protestant community and even
build—to be truthful, on the outskirts—a church and
a bishop's palace. And, imagine that, I wrangled some
money from the government for it.

In terms of our mutual friends and their fates, things
went like this: Lama Tikhonov withdrew with the
Red Army; he could not stand the democratization of
Mongolia. And up to a point, he was right: democracy
and religion go together like oil and water. As far as I've
heard, he grew disappointed in Buddhism and is now an
activist in the "Pamjat" Russian Nationalist Party. And
Chuck, Chuck got a promotion. The new government
appointed him as the editor in chief of the Ulaanbaatar

newspaper for foreigners, The Ulaanbaatar Weekly. We drank a lot of whiskey together (now one drinks whiskey there), recalling you and Mr. Mercier, before—in the same way I arrived in Mongolia—I reappeared in Amsterdam.

Once, I read an interesting sentence in Fuentes (which, by the way, you could use as the epigraph of some future novel): "But reason—neither slow nor indolent—tells us that merely with repetition the extraordinary becomes ordinary, and, only briefly abandoned, what had once passed for a common and ordinary occurrence becomes a portent."

I think that the secret of my return to Amsterdam lies there. As long as I was confused and afraid because of my diplomatic and oneiric status, I lost faith in myself and committed one mistake after another. When I made peace with my fate and organized my life, when I melded into the ordinary and began to make plans for the future, one evening I fell asleep and, after all that time, I dreamt that I was in my office in Amsterdam. Well, when I was supposed to wake up, I felt tired and lay down on the couch.

And I woke up again in Amsterdam. "This dream is really lasting a long time," I thought, but I simply could not wake up. In the end, I gave up. Now I am here, and I have taken up my duties again. Only from time to time, more out of nostalgia than doubt, I pause for one of my afternoon walks along the canal and wonder: were all the things that happened in Mongolia my dream, or yours?

SOKOL CLUB IN PRISHTINA

No. 55

June 1929

TO OUR BROTHER PRESIDENT OF THE
MUNICIPALITY

TO OUR BROTHER SOKOL CLUB IN
KRUŠEVAC

On June 18 this year, the Cyclist Section of the
Sokol Club in Prishtina is setting off on a staged tour
from Prishtina (Kosovo) to Dubrovnik. We are taking the liberty to ask you in a brotherly way to aide
this section so that they can more easily find room
and board for the short time they will be in your
town.

The section has 10 members (males) under the
leadership of our brother Principal, a high school
teacher.

Hoping that you will respond to our humble
request in brotherly fashion, we greet you with a
brotherly

REGARDS

About the day of arrival, we will inform you ahead of
time by telegraph

SECRETARY   WARDEN
(Signature illegible)   (Signature illegible)

June 3, 1929
HEADQUARTERS COLONEL
Prishtina

ROUTE: Priština—Kosovska Mitrovica—Peć—Andrijevica—Podgorica—Cetinje—Kotor—Dubrovnik—Mostar—Sarajevo—Užice—Čačak—Kruševac—Aleksinac—Niš—Vranje—Kumanovo.

Selected Dalkey Archive Paperbacks

www.dalkeyarchive.com